"I can't believe you found the experience so—so unforgettable."

"Don't make fun of me, Beth," he warned, and for the first time since that night at the flat, she feared the consequences of her actions. "It was good between us. More than good, damn you, for all your crazy games!"

"*My* games!"

"Well, what would you call them?" he demanded huskily, grasping her wrists and pulling them behind her back. "What else would drive an apparently sober-minded academic to act like a cheap tart?"

"Alex, isn't this rather childish? Let me go, please!"

"That's not what you said that night," he taunted. "As I remember, you were desperate for my body. Desperate for me to touch you..."

ANNE MATHER began her career by writing the kind of book she likes to read—romance. Married, with two children, this author from the north of England has become a favorite with readers of romance fiction around the world. In addition to writing, Anne enjoys reading, driving and traveling to locations that often become the settings for new novels.

Books by Anne Mather

STORMSPELL
WILD CONCERTO
HIDDEN IN THE FLAME
THE LONGEST PLEASURE

HARLEQUIN PRESENTS PLUS

1567—RICH AS SIN
1591—TIDEWATER SEDUCTION

HARLEQUIN PRESENTS

1492—BETRAYED
1514—DIAMOND FIRE
1542—GUILTY
1553—DANGEROUS SANCTUARY
1617—SNOWFIRE
1649—TENDER ASSAULT

Anne Mather
A Secret Rebellion

Harlequin Books

TORONTO • NEW YORK • LONDON
AMSTERDAM • PARIS • SYDNEY • HAMBURG
STOCKHOLM • ATHENS • TOKYO • MILAN
MADRID • WARSAW • BUDAPEST • AUCKLAND

ISBN 0-373-11663-2

A SECRET REBELLION

Copyright © 1993 by Anne Mather.

This edition published by arrangement with Harlequin Enterprises B. V.

® and TM are trademarks of the publisher. Trademarks indicated with ® are registered in the United States Patent and Trademark Office, the Canadian Trade Marks Office and in other countries.

Printed in U.S.A.

PROLOGUE

ALEX noticed her as soon as she came into the room.

He had been standing in the broad bay of the window, a glass of some obnoxious liquid in his hand, wondering how soon he could decently make his excuses and leave. Gatherings like this were not his scene, and he had only agreed to come because it was his nephew's birthday, and someone had to represent the family. Or at least that was his father's excuse. In any other circumstances, he would have refused, but the old man was unwell, and for once Alex had been persuaded to do his bidding.

Consequently, it was not surprising that his restless gaze should alight on the one woman at the party who wasn't underdressed. For the past hour—was it only an hour?—he had been discouraging the advances of a parade of females, in most cases young enough to be his daughter, all of whom seemed to consider it necessary to wear as little as possible. That was why the newcomer's appearance, in a plain black dress, was so startling. Among this crowd she stood out like the raven at the feast.

Not that the dress itself was unattractive, he amended, with a critical frown. The neckline was modest, but appealing, and her skirt ended several inches above her knee. Of course, the fact that she was also wearing opaque black tights added to the illusion of propriety. And only the fact that the light was behind her revealed the length and beauty of her legs.

It hadn't occurred to him that he had ignored her face. In truth, he wasn't much interested in anything except the unusual mode of her appearance. He'd registered that she was fairly tall, and slim, and that she evidently dressed with some regard for the weather. Outside the

5

apartment, the temperature was dipping to somewhere near freezing point.

Alex propped his shoulder more comfortably against the wall, and looked down into his glass. The drink it contained was a curious greenish colour. His nephew's girlfriend—what was her name? Christina?—had informed him it was punch, but it didn't taste like it to him. He must be getting old. He would have much preferred Scotch, or even the spirit he had been weaned on. These designer drinks were all very well, but he had no intention of risking a driving violation.

'Hi.'

The casual overture arrested the downward spiral of his thoughts, but he had physically to steel himself to face the confrontation civilly. To hell with it, he thought; as soon as he could find Nick, he was getting out of here. He'd shown his face; he'd done his duty. If his nephew didn't like it, then that was his hard luck.

He lifted his head slowly, preparing himself to face yet another unsubtle come-on, and then felt his focus shifting. The young woman who had issued the friendly greeting was the woman in black, as he had mentally dubbed her, the newcomer, whose appearance had so compulsively drawn his attention.

'Um—hi,' he offered politely, realising he had done her an injustice by ignoring her pale features. She was quite startlingly good-looking, and although she might not fit his normal assessment of what made a woman beautiful her face was none the less worthy of approval.

'You don't mind if I join you, do you?' she added, and although Alex had been determined not to get involved in any pointless exchange he found himself shaking his head, as if in acknowledgement of her proposition. 'I thought you looked lonely,' she added, her lips parting to display white, white teeth. And, although he had heard that line half a dozen times already that evening, from her it actually sounded sincere.

'Bored,' he amended drily, and then, remembering his manners, 'I'm sorry. I didn't mean to sound rude.'

She smiled, and Alex was struck again by the flawless delicacy of her beauty. She was very fair, of course. Much different from the women of his family. And with pale skin, and deep blue eyes, she could not have displayed a greater contrast to his own swarthy appearance.

But, as he acknowledged the narrow cheekbones, and straight, unblemished nose, the wide, sensual mouth, and small but determined chin, Alex couldn't help wondering what she was doing with him. With long lashes, several shades darker than her silvery cap of hair, and a slim, yet not unshapely figure, she could have approached any man in the room, and not been repulsed. In fact, he found her comparatively modest style of clothing unexpectedly sexy, among so much exposed flesh. And, judging by the glances she was getting, he wasn't the only man to think so.

Which brought him back to his original query as to why she should have made a bee-line for him. It wasn't as if he had encouraged her. Dammit, he hadn't even looked at her, until she spoke to him. And it couldn't be his appearance. In worn jeans and a leather jacket, he looked little different from a dozen other males in the room, and decidedly older.

Unless...

'I must admit I don't like parties much either,' she said ruefully, interrupting his train of thought. She indicated the glass she was holding and which contained an identical concoction to his own, and grimaced. 'What do you think this is? Moonshine?'

Alex found his lips twitching. 'I wish it were,' he replied, pulling a similar face. 'Cat's you-know-what is my guess. I'd suggest you treat it cautiously.'

'Oh, I will.'

Her laughter was infectious, and several pairs of eyes turned in their direction. Including his nephew's, Alex noticed. He hoped Nick didn't think he had orchestrated this encounter.

'What's your name?'

Her question was not unexpected, and Alex dragged his eyes away from her smiling mouth, and endeavoured to give it serious consideration. But he was unwillingly aware of a certain disappointment. If she knew who he was, all his questions would be answered.

'I—Alex,' he said, after a moment's hesitation. 'Alex—Th—Thorpe.'

'Nice name.' Her response was guileless, as far as he could tell, and there had been no glimmer of suspicion in those wide indigo eyes. 'I'm Elizabeth Ryan.' She held out her hand. 'How do you do?'

Alex took her hand in his much larger one, noticing the contrast between her flesh and his. And he was irritably aware of his own reaction to the contact. Her skin was as smooth and soft as silk, and he wanted to hold on.

Amazingly enough, she seemed to feel the same. Even though he held her hand far longer than was necessary she made no move to pull away. On the contrary, she looked up at him with a curiously satisfied look in her disturbing eyes, and Alex had the distinct impression that she was well aware of his response.

In the event, he broke the contact, thrusting his hand into the back pocket of his jeans, as if to remove it as far as possible from danger. *Danger*? He took a less than cautious swig of the punch in his glass, and swallowed the oath that sprang unguarded to his lips. God, this stuff must be stronger than he thought, he chided himself harshly. It was years since he had felt so—aroused.

'So who do you know?' she asked, sipping her own drink, and then pulling a face, and Alex frowned.

'I beg your——?'

'Nick or Christina,' she prompted, moving out of the way of a couple, who were performing a rather heavy-footed version of the lambada. 'I work with Chris, and I don't believe she's mentioned you before.'

'No.' Alex endeavoured to soften his stiff features. 'No, I—know Nick. Um—from way back.'

'I see.' She nodded, glancing round at the thickening crowd that was filling the living-room of the apartment. 'I must admit, I didn't realise Chris had asked so many people. I wonder if they all had an invitation?' Her lips parted, giving him another tantalising glimpse of her tongue. 'Probably not. But who's going to ask if they're gatecrashers?'

'Well, not me,' remarked Alex drily, and she laughed.

'Me, neither,' she agreed, and as she moved back again her hip brushed the taut muscles of his thigh.

He could smell her now. The faintly musky fragrance she was wearing filled his senses, and combined with the indefinable femininity of her body. Her hair smelt deliciously of lemon, and where it turned into her nape it was inclined to curl. It was short hair, straight, but expertly cut. It framed her face quite delightfully, and she had a habit of pushing her fingers through it. Alex thought he would like to push his fingers through it too, before he could stifle the impulse. For even though it clung silkily to her fingers it always returned to its original shape.

He was crazy, he told himself severely. It was long past the time when he had intended to get out of here, and he ought to make a move. Before her—Elizabeth's—arrival, he had been itching to make his excuses and leave. Yet now he was reluctant to do so.

He could imagine what his father would say if he knew why Alex was delaying his departure. The old man had asked him to come here to keep an eye on Nick, for God's sake. His nephew was known to be reckless, and too impressionable for his own good. And, although the family were prepared to tolerate his relationship with Christina Lennox, no one was in any doubt that he would eventually marry the girl his grandfather had chosen for him.

It didn't matter that Alex thought his father had rather too much to say where his grandsons were concerned. It was the way things were done in his family, but—please God!—he'd never get like that. Yet with his brother too ineffectual to stand against the old man's wishes, it was usually left to Alex to play devil's advocate. It was not a role that lay comfortably on his shoulders, and as far as Tony was concerned he played it far too well. But that was why he was here tonight: to provide a stabilising influence. Not find himself attracted to a woman who was not only unsuitable, but whom he didn't even know.

'Have you eaten?'

The words were out before he could prevent them, and the young woman looked up at him with warm enquiring eyes. 'No,' she said. 'No, actually, I haven't. But I expect there's some food around here somewhere. I think Chris said something about a buffet.'

It was his let-out, but he didn't take it. 'I meant, would you like to get out of here, and find some place where we could have supper?' he explained. He indicated the smoke-laden atmosphere. 'I don't know about you, but I could stand some fresh air.'

'Oh.' Elizabeth appeared to give his invitation some thought. 'Well—I'm not sure——'

'I'm quite respectable,' he offered, realising he had never done anything so impulsive in his life. 'And I do mean supper. It's not an unsubtle excuse to get you into bed.'

She smiled. 'Isn't it?' And he felt the incredible awareness of heat invading his neck. 'Oh, well, I'll have to make do with supper, then, won't I? Give me a minute, and I'll go and tell Chris what's going on.'

His nephew was not unnaturally shocked to hear why he was leaving. 'You're taking a strange woman to supper!' he exclaimed, staring at Alex as if he'd suddenly grown two heads. 'So—who is she? Tell me. Do I know her? Good God, I can't believe you're doing this!'

'Her name is Elizabeth Ryan, and she's a friend of Christina's,' declared Alex flatly. 'And I'm only taking her for something to eat. Nothing else.'

'I should hope not.' Nick's dark eyes were frankly amazed. 'Does she know who you are? Have you told her?'

'She knows I am a man who has offered to buy her a meal.' Alex was dismissive. 'That's enough.'

'But if she knows——'

'She doesn't.'

'How can you be sure?'

'I am not offering her marriage, Nico.' Alex sighed. 'Do not concern yourself with my morals. You are too young to give advice to someone old enough to be your father!'

'Hardly that.' Nick was indignant.

'Oh, I think so,' responded Alex lazily. 'I was a very mature teenager.' He cuffed his nephew on the shoulder. 'Enjoy yourself, Nico. With God's grace I should see you in the morning.'

Elizabeth was waiting for him in the foyer. She had put on a dark green raincoat that almost reached her ankles, and knee-length boots that disappeared beneath the hem. She was certainly prepared for the weather, he reflected. Only her silvery head was uncovered.

She ran her fingers through her hair as he came towards her. It occurred to him that it was a faintly nervous gesture. And why not? he asked himself, zipping up his jacket. She knew even less about him than he did about her.

'Did you find Christina?' he asked, leaning past her to open the door, and for a moment her expression was blank.

Then, 'Chris? Oh—yes.' He stood back and she hurried into the hall outside. 'Mmm, it's chilly. Are you sure you'll be warm enough without an overcoat?'

Alex closed the door behind them, and pulled a wry face. As he went everywhere by car, he seldom considered the weather. But it was possible she didn't have a car. That she used the bus or the Underground. And his appearance had evidently not led her to believe he was particularly affluent.

He frowned, as the realisation that she would soon know quite a lot more about him surfaced. It had been easy enough maintaining his anonymity in Nick's girlfriend's apartment. At least half the men present had been wearing jeans and casual jackets. But how many of them had come here in a year-old Ferrari?

As they went down the stairs and out into the chill of a March evening, Alex examined his alternatives. He could pretend he had had too much to drink and suggest they hail a cab. It shouldn't be too difficult to find a cruising taxi on the Embankment, and Christina's apartment was only a stone's throw from there. Indeed, Alex had been relieved to find her address was in a reasonably respectable part of the city. There were areas of London where he'd have had some hesitation at leaving his car unattended.

Or, he could suggest they walk along the Strand, where they were bound to find a suitable restaurant. In fact, he knew of an Italian establishment just off William Street, where they served the juiciest pizzas he had ever tasted.

Or, and it was probably the most sensible, whatever his misgivings, he could collect his car, and drive to a decent hotel that provided valet parking. He could always pretend he was looking after the car for a friend—if indeed she knew anything about Italian sports cars.

'My car's over here.'

For a moment, he thought he had said the words, but almost immediately he realised he hadn't. Elizabeth was indicating a dark blue Peugeot, parked precisely in front of a dark green Ferrari, and Alex allowed his breath to escape an a rueful sigh. Evidently, she had chosen to take charge of their transportation, and, while it solved his problem, he felt a fleeting sense of regret at having the decision taken out of his hands.

She unlocked the car as he walked round to the passenger side. He chose to walk round the back of the car, running his fingers regretfully over the Ferrari's grille. Whatever happened to male domination? he wondered drily. Still, at least it would save him the trouble of taking her home afterwards.

The passenger seat was too far forward, and his knees nudged the dashboard. 'Make yourself comfortable. That seat's seldom used,' she advised him easily. Then, looking through her rear-view mirror, 'Goodness, why do people park so close to the boot? I've hardly got enough room to get out of here.'

Alex deliberately refrained from glancing over his shoulder. He knew exactly how close the Ferrari was. 'Shortage of space, I guess,' he volunteered lightly, and she muttered something about power-steering as she manoeuvred out into the traffic.

It was cold in the car, and the windows were misted with their breath, but she seemed to know where she was going. Alex wondered if she was going to ask him where they ought to park, but then decided she probably knew the city better than he did. He was all right in the well-lit streets and main thoroughfares, but when it came to negotiating its one-way system he was soon in trouble.

The heater began working as they drove along the Embankment, and the windows started to clear. It meant he had more light to see the delicate curve of her profile, and the determined way she held her tongue between her teeth when she was concentrating. He still couldn't get over the fact that he had actually invited her to have dinner with him. Nick was right. It wasn't like him. Dear God, what kind of a woman was she, to leave the party with a man she had only just met?

He was so busy thinking about his reasons, and hers, that he was paying little attention to their surroundings. He had assumed she knew a short cut to the West End. He knew, because he had done it, that it was possible to run up one of these streets into Whitehall, or Piccadilly. He had expected her to do that. But he suddenly realised they were crossing the river, and that was not the way to reach their destination.

Alarm flickered along his veins, but it was only a momentary thing. He knew he was perfectly capable of overpowering her, any time he chose, and that if this was some crazy attempt at kidnapping she had chosen the wrong man. But what if she had accomplices? What if when she stopped there were a couple of hoodlums waiting for him? He ought to do something now, before he lost the initiative.

But, before he could marshal any defence, Elizabeth braked, and turned the car into a narrow street of tall Victorian houses. 'Nearly there,' she said, turning and giving him a winsome smile, and he had the uneasy suspicion that she knew exactly what he was thinking.

'Nearly where?' he responded, his tone much less cordial than hers, and she tucked her lower lip between her teeth.

'My apartment,' she replied, braking again, as she swung the Peugeot over to the kerb. There was just room for her to squeeze the little saloon between a dust-smeared Renault and an ancient convertible. 'I thought I'd cook you supper. Do you mind?'

Alex stared at her. 'You!'

'Hmm, me,' she agreed, putting the car into neutral, and turning off the engine. 'Believe it or not, but I can cook. Nothing fancy, you understand, but good wholesome food.'

Alex didn't know whether to laugh or give her a piece of his mind. It was his own fault, of course. If he hadn't been so ambivalent about revealing that he owned a Ferrari, he'd have been in control. As it was, she had taken events into her own hands, and he could either like it or do the other thing.

He shook his head. He could always call a cab, he supposed. But that would definitely seem ungracious. And, after all, it didn't really matter where they ate. If she was prepared to invite a stranger into her home, why should he grumble?

'Are you serious?' he asked, putting his hand on the door-handle, and she nodded.

'Of course.' She licked lips that suddenly looked a little uncertain. 'You're not a rapist or anything, are you?'

Alex grimaced. 'Would I tell you, if I were?'

Elizabeth bit her lip. 'I suppose not.'

'Well, I'm not,' said Alex shortly, thrusting open his door. 'Come on. It's too cold to sit here discussing my sexual habits.' He grinned. 'We can do that much more comfortably inside, hmm?'

Elizabeth got out, but she still looked uncertain. 'I have neighbours,' she informed him. 'If I screamed——'

'Oh, please.' Alex spread his hands. 'I'm not a rapist. Nor do I prey on lonely women. Now, can we go inside?'

Her apartment was on the third floor, and Alex groaned as they reached the landing. 'Someone ought to teach the English to install elevators in their apartment buildings!' he exclaimed, leaning against the wall, as she searched for her keys. 'This is the seventh flight of stairs I've climbed tonight!'

She frowned. 'You said—*the* English; aren't you English?'

Alex could have bitten out his tongue. 'Half,' he said, hoping she wouldn't ask what the other half was. The door opened, and he followed her inside. 'Hmm, this is—nice.'

'It's awful,' she assured him fervently, closing the door and securing the lock. 'But—it's rented. The furniture, too. It's practically impossible to rent a decent apartment in London without its being furnished.'

'Hmm.' Alex pushed his hands into the back pockets of his jeans and looked about him, as he followed her into a lamplit living-room. Happily, she seemed to have been diverted from asking about his nationality, and he was more than willing to keep her talking about the apartment if that would do the trick. 'Do you live here alone?'

She looked at him quickly and then away. 'I—yes,' she replied, shedding her raincoat on to a chintz-covered sofa, and stepping into the tiny kitchen, which opened off the living-room. She switched on a track of spotlights. 'So—what would you like to eat? I've got steak, chicken, frozen pizza? Or I could scramble us some eggs.'

Alex propped his hip against the fixture. 'Frozen pizza sounds good to me,' he declared, choosing the one that required the least preparation. He had noticed the microwave oven standing at one end of the Formica-topped counter, and he had prepared himself enough frozen meals to know it was a simple matter to defrost and cook the pizza. 'How about you?'

'Mmm. That sounds good to me, too,' she agreed, bending to take the box from the freezer. 'Er—it's cheese and tomato. Is that all right?'

'Whatever.' Alex turned away from the sight of her neatly rounded buttocks, and the way her skirt rode halfway up her thighs as she bent over. It exposed the fact that she wasn't wearing tights at all, but black stockings, and the unexpected glimpse of her inner thigh, soft, and smooth, and creamy white, was more disturbing than he wanted it to be. 'So——' he endeavoured to school his racing pulse '—what do you do for a living?'

She put the pizza into the microwave before replying, and then came to the end of the counter, and propped her elbows on it. 'What do you think I do?'

'I don't know.' Alex turned, raking back his dark hair with a slightly impatient hand. He shrugged. 'Something glamorous, I suppose. Modelling, perhaps.'

She laughed. 'As in artist's?'

'As in fashion,' amended Alex shortly, not appreciating her humour. 'I assumed you had a job where looks played a part.'

'Is that a compliment?'

Alex's mouth compressed. 'If you want it to be.'

She hesitated. 'All right. So I'm—involved in fashion. But not as a model. I—buy clothes.'

'A fashion buyer?'

'Mmm.' She seemed content with that description. 'Now can I offer you a drink?'

Alex thought about saying no, because he was driving, and then thought better of it. He had only had one glass of that appalling punch at the party, and right now he could use something stronger. Preferably whisky, he thought grimly. At this moment, he was feeling at a decided disadvantage.

'What have you got?' he asked, and she turned away to take a bottle of Scotch out of one of the cupboards.

'Only this, I'm afraid,' she said, not realising how relieved Alex was feeling. It was much later when he conceived the thought that Chivas Regal was hardly the expected thing to find in a single woman's apartment.

He took it straight, with ice, and after she had settled him on the sofa she returned to the kitchen. She hardly touched her own drink, he noticed. But that was hardly surprising, considering she had practically drowned the Scotch with water.

'Do you work in London?'

Her question caught him unawares, and Alex took refuge in his drink before replying. 'Partly,' he admitted, at last, realising he didn't have to lie about his whereabouts. London was pretty big, after all.

'Partly?' She left the salad she had been mixing, and came to the end of the counter again. 'What does that mean?'

'Oh...' Alex floundered, realising that instead of concentrating on an answer he was looking at her breasts. She had unusually full breasts, and they had been thrown into prominence by the position of the spotlights. They were probably the reason she wasn't a model, he reflected. Although she was slim, her breasts and hips were much too generously rounded. 'I mean—I travel, too. Quite a lot,' he appended, deciding the whisky was responsible for the thickness of his tongue. 'You know what travelling salesmen are like—here today and there tomorrow.'

Much to his dismay, she picked up the bottle of Scotch, and came to refill his glass. 'Really,' she said, bending over him, and he was intensely aware that she wasn't wearing a bra. Not that she really needed one, he conceded, imagining how she would look without the confining fabric of her dress. Which begged the thought of whether she was wearing any underwear at all, and he cradled his glass between his hands in case he was tempted to find out.

The trouble was, he had the distinct suspicion that she wouldn't object if he did so. God, what kind of woman was she? She looked so innocent, but she was acting like a—a——

The actual word he wanted to use escaped him. Besides, if he was completely honest with himself he would admit that apart from bringing him here she'd done nothing to incite his sexuality. Except inflame his senses, he thought impatiently. Good God, every move she made set his nerves on edge.

'So what do you sell?' she asked, and he breathed a little easier, as she moved back into the kitchen.

But the question still needed answering, and, taking another mouthful of Scotch, he conceived the perfect answer. 'Oil,' he replied, feeling pleased with himself. 'Um—olive oil.' That was better. 'We import it from Greece.' He grinned suddenly, enjoying his own joke. 'Barrels and barrels of it.'

'Gosh.'

She sounded really interested, and just for a moment he felt a heel. But, dammit, he didn't know her from Adam—or Eve; he grimaced. And after this evening there was every chance that he'd never see her again.

The apartment was getting warm now, and looking round he decided it wasn't as ugly as he had at first thought. The lamps cast a mellow shadow over the worn patches in the carpet, and even the picture of the oriental lady over the fireplace had taken on a hazy luminescence.

Taking off his jacket, he laid it over the back of the sofa, and lounged a little lower on the cushions. It was really rather pleasant, he thought, sitting here, talking to a beautiful woman, smelling the scent of the pizza sizzling in the oven. He relaxed, savouring the flavour of the whisky. He didn't know why he had been apprehensive.

And, almost inevitably, it seemed, his eyes were drawn back to Elizabeth. He liked watching her. He liked the way she moved. And he liked the way the light reflected off her hair. She looked both innocent and knowing, and he was growing less and less immune to her undoubted sensuality.

He swallowed more of the Chivas, and lifted his foot to rest his ankle across his knee. Think of something else, he ordered himself, resisting the urge to look at her again, but the awareness of her nearness was causing his blood to thicken. It throbbed in his head, with an urgency that brought an actual physical ache, but the core of that ache was centred somewhere else entirely.

'Have some more whisky,' she murmured, and he realised she had left the kitchen and was standing beside the couch. Her hand was outstretched, on the point of pouring more of the potent spirit into his glass, and only his swift withdrawal prevented her from achieving her objective.

'Are you trying to get me drunk?' he demanded harshly, as his brain struggled to come to terms with what was happening. What did she want of him? Why *had* she brought him here?

She smiled then, setting the whisky aside, and sitting down on the couch beside him. As she did so, she allowed her body to slide against him, and Alex felt the jolt of that contact firing every nerve he possessed.

'Would you mind if I were?' she asked, and it took Alex a moment to comprehend what she was talking about.

'That depends why you're doing it,' he said, his eyes drawn to the moistness of her lower lip. 'I can't believe it's because you want my body. A woman like you—you wouldn't have to get a man drunk to——' He broke off, his lips twisting. 'But you know what I'm talking about, don't you?'

'Do I?' Her tongue appeared again. 'Tell me. I like it when you talk dirty.'

Alex grimaced. 'Lady, I'm not talking dirty, believe me.'

'Thinking dirty, then,' she amended, pressing one long finger against her lips. 'Tell me what you're thinking. I want to know. You do like me, don't you?'

Alex swallowed. 'You're crazy!'

'Why?' She removed her finger from her lips and drew it down his dark-skinned cheek. 'Because I want to know what you really think about me?' Her eyes were wide and innocent. 'Do you want to kiss me?'

Alex's head felt as if it was about to explode. And not just his head, he admitted grimly. The zip of his jeans felt as if it was in danger of disintegrating, as the smouldering heat in his body spread down into the cradle of his sex.

'That's beside the point,' he said stiffly, struggling to combat his rising passion. God, if she didn't move away soon, he'd very likely lose the battle, and, aroused as he was, could he be relied on to do the right thing?

'Is it?' she persisted, leaning towards him, so that those glorious breasts were pressed against his arm. 'I think that means you do. So why don't you?'

Alex caught his breath. 'I think I heard the microwave switch off,' he muttered. 'Don't you think you ought to take a look at the pizza?'

'I'd rather look at you,' she responded, sliding her soft hand along his cheek. 'Mmm, that's rough. I bet you need to shave at least twice a day.'

'Elizabeth——'

'Liz.'

'Liz, then——' Her other hand was on his thigh now, cupped over the muscles that stretched above his knee. 'Let's not rush things, shall we?'

Her eyes darkened. 'You don't like me?'

He stifled an oath. 'Of course I like you——'

'Well, then . . .' She looked at him with those deep indigo eyes. 'So long as we understand one another.' One finger performed a circular movement against his leg. 'I think we should have another drink.'

'No.' Alex managed to get the word out with an effort. He had drunk far too much whisky as it was. Looking down at her hand, for instance, he knew he should remove it. The trouble was his brain couldn't formulate the message.

'I saw you looking at me, you know,' she murmured, and for a moment his mind was a blank. 'At the party,' she added, offering him illumination. 'I saw you the minute I arrived. You're quite—noticeable. Big—and dark—and sexy.'

Alex tried for a laugh. 'Who? Me? With this ugly mug? I think you've got the wrong guy.'

'No, I haven't.' She gazed at him intently. 'You're not ugly and you know it. I bet you've known a lot of women, haven't you?'

Alex drew an uneven breath. 'Not as many as you think.'

She frowned. 'Are you married?'

Not any more. 'No.'

'That's good.' She seemed to breathe a little more easily, and he wondered why it mattered to her. If she was what he thought she was, whether he was married or not shouldn't be an issue. 'Can I kiss you?'

Alex felt like a youth on his first date. For God's sake, he was too old for this, he thought, so what was he doing here? Whatever she wanted, he would be very unwise to linger. He wasn't the kind of man who carried protection around as a matter of course.

Her perfume assaulted his senses as her tongue brushed his parted lips. It was a potent mix of some expensive fragrance, combined with the warm, womanly smell of her body. It was a long time since he had been aroused by the mere scent of a woman, but he felt his senses swimming as she rubbed herself against him.

'Nice,' she breathed, against his mouth, and Alex knew his actions were slipping out of control. Her hand against his thigh was a constant torment, and, thrusting the whisky glass on the floor, he grasped her shoulders.

Afterwards he couldn't remember what he had intended to do. He thought perhaps he had tried to push her away, but all he had succeeded in doing was dragging her closer. With his senses running riot, he ground his lips against hers, delivering hard, hungry kisses to her moist, willing mouth.

And her mouth was so amazingly desirable. Hot, and urgent, and deliciously receptive, her lips parting easily to accommodate his possession. He had never kissed anyone who responded so completely, and he thought he might burn in the fire of her touch.

He heard the tremulous little moan she gave as his tongue plunged into her mouth, but it was hardly a protest. With one hand clinging to the back of his neck, and the other trapped between his legs, she was totally aware of what she was doing. It was Alex who had the distinct impression he was being manipulated, but the thunder of his blood made him deaf to any warning.

His hands moved over her back, confirming his belief that she wasn't wearing a bra. They also found the tab of the zip that ran from the high neck at the back of the dress to her hips. With an effort, he controlled the urge to tear the dress off her, and allowed his fingers to gently part the teeth.

She shivered when his hands invaded the opened back of the dress and, just for a moment, he sensed a certain unwillingness to continue. But, dammit, it was too late for her to be having second thoughts now, he decided grimly. She had asked for this, and she couldn't blame him for taking her at her word.

Her spine was straight and slender, the skin smooth and soft as silk. When he allowed his fingers to follow its line, she arched automatically against him. And when his exploration found the lacy edge of her panties she sucked in her breath with a gulp.

So, she was wearing underwear, he acknowledged, in some distant corner of his mind, far removed from the immediacy of what he was doing. Not totally shameless, then, and perhaps a little inexperienced. But she didn't try to stop him, when he inserted his finger and found the tender cleft that quivered beneath.

However, these thoughts only registered at a subconscious level. The actual recklessness of what he was doing, and the realisation that he might be risking life and limb just to get laid, couldn't seem to penetrate the swirling fog of his passion. Her mouth, her skin, the tantalising delights of her body still to be uncovered, seemed far more important than some possible threat of infection. Whether it was the whisky or not, he was at the mercy of his own needs, and when she took his hand, and got up from the couch, he followed her instinctively.

She didn't turn a lamp on in the bedroom, but the light from the living-room provided a shadowy illumination. And, when she peeled the black dress down her body, taking her panties with it, exposing herself in only black stockings and suspenders, the luminous quality of her skin was all the light he needed.

He wanted to worship her body. She was so beautiful, so exquisite, that anything less seemed a crime. But when she came to him, and began unbuckling his belt, he knew he had to have her. With or without her participation, he desperately needed to bury himself in her body.

He tore off his shirt and jeans with hands he knew were trembling. God, he chided himself, he *was* like a callow youth, frantic for his first initiation. What was wrong with him, for pity's sake? It wasn't as if he'd never wanted a woman before. But not as much as he wanted this one, a small voice warned him, as she backed up on to the bed, coiling one long leg under her and drawing up her other knee. Every move she made excited him, and his eyes were drawn to the glimpse of blonde curls, just visible behind her updrawn thigh. God, he thought unsteadily, she was good. She knew exactly how to tantalise his senses.

But it was her breasts he caressed first, as he came down on the bed beside her. They were just as glorious as he had imagined, and she let him weigh them in his hands, before carrying the swollen nipples to his lips. He suckled greedily, feeling the ache of his arousal hard against her thigh. Soon, very soon, he promised himself with feeling, aware that he was fast approaching the point of no return.

But he noticed, almost in passing, that she kept her eyes fixed on him, and what he was doing to her body. She never once looked down at his manhood, rearing beside her hip. And he wanted her to. He knew a sudden urgent need for her to do so. He wanted her to touch him, as he was touching her.

It was almost his undoing. When he took her hand, and brought it down to his throbbing heated flesh, he shuddered helplessly. The headlong rush of excitement he felt when her slim cool fingers curled about him was beyond belief. He knew, if he weren't careful, he'd spill himself into her hands.

'It's so big,' he heard her whisper, and even though his mind was spinning out of his grasp he couldn't prevent the hoarse laugh that escaped his throat. But not for long, he thought, with grim humour, aware of his own limitations. He couldn't wait to feel the heat when her tight sheath closed about him.

He tipped her back against the pillows, and buried his face between her breasts. Then, trailing kisses from her throat to her navel, he found the lace-trimmed edge of her suspenders. He propped himself on one elbow, and thought how deliciously sinful she looked wearing only her stockings. To hell with it, he thought, pressing his face to the hollow planes of her stomach. He'd dispose of them later, after he'd eased his aching flesh.

He stroked his hand along the outside of her thigh, and then probed the parting of her legs. Only they weren't apart, he discovered; they were clamped tightly together; and when he eased his hand between the muscles jerked uncontrollably.

So, not so experienced at all, he realised, feeling the tangible flexing of the flesh. But more appealing than any blatant invitation. And it didn't take long for him to persuade her to let him have his way.

She was ready for him. However nervous she might outwardly appear, her body was prepared for his invasion. When he probed the moist curls and found the tender nub of her femininity, she jerked helplessly against his fingers, and when he removed his hand, and rubbed himself against her, her breath came quick and fast against his chest.

Alex couldn't wait any longer. He was not a man who normally satisfied himself at the expense of his partner, but right now he was too aroused to hold back. Nudging her legs apart with one hairy thigh, he positioned himself between them, bringing her hand down to guide him into her moist responsive core.

Her breathing was practically non-existent when she reached for him, and her judgement was little better as she struggled to do what he wanted. In the end, Alex brushed her hand aside and found his own destiny, thrusting himself into her with a gentle, yet forceful motion.

She was tight, so tight it hurt, but it was too late to recognise what he should have recognised sooner. Besides, as soon as he felt her taut muscles close about him, his body convulsed. She was so beautiful, so desirable, and he groaned as his long-awaited release burst from him.

'You should have told me,' he muttered, when he was able to talk again, but although he had expected to find tears on her cheeks she looked remarkably composed when he drew back to look down at her.

'Does it matter?' she asked, looking up at him, her eyes shadowy in the subdued light, and in the aftermath of such a soul-shattering experience Alex was inclined to be philosophical. Given his quite amazing desire for her, he doubted he could have drawn back anyway, and even lying here, supposedly relaxed, he was still heavily aware of her perfection.

'That depends,' he said now, as he had said earlier in the evening, smoothing her cheeks with his thumbs, 'what you expect of me.'

She smiled then. 'Just your body,' she assured him, with staggering confidence. 'Now, may I get up? I ought to see to the pizza.'

'Not yet.'

Alex's lips twisted, as he felt himself growing hard again. Even after the discovery that she had been a virgin—or, perhaps, because of it—he found he had a definite proprietorial interest in her body, and even though her eyes were vaguely anxious now he was loath to let her go.

'You—can't,' she protested, but the awareness she suddenly exhibited, proved that she knew he could.

'Let's see, shall we?' he breathed, his thumb invading her parted lips. 'Just for the fun of it...'

CHAPTER ONE

SO, SHE was pregnant.

Beth came out of the private clinic, and stood for several minutes on the pavement, letting the warm breeze of the May morning fan her hot temples. Then, after taking a deep breath, she tucked her bag beneath her arm, and started along the quiet street to where she had left her car.

It was curious. She had thought she would feel different somehow. Not triumphant, exactly, but certainly content that her plan had proved fruitful. It was what she had wanted, what she had aimed for. So why did she suddenly feel so hollow?

She needed something to eat, she decided. She'd noticed a distinct increase in her appetite lately, and, although she didn't believe the old maxim that she was eating for two, she had found that smaller and more frequent intakes of food helped to keep the nausea at bay.

The small Renault was airless, and she wound down all the windows before inserting her key in the ignition. The car had been standing in the sun for over an hour, and the seat was warm beneath the short skirt of her formal suit.

Before starting the engine, she tipped the rear-view mirror towards her, and examined her face rather critically. She didn't look any different, she thought, but that was hardly surprising. Nothing momentous had happened that morning. The event which had changed her life had occurred more than eight weeks ago, in another time and another place. That was when she might have expected to see some radical alteration in her appearance. That morning, when she had fled from the

London apartment, leaving Alex Thorpe still asleep, and totally unaware of the deception she had practised on him.

There was a certain guilty awareness in her eyes now, eyes that in sunlight were more violet than indigo. But, for heaven's sake, she had taken nothing from him. It was he who had done the taking, and if he had left something in return then that was only fair, wasn't it?

She expelled a breath, and turned the mirror away from her flushed features. The fact that the becoming blush of colour added a delicate definition to her high cheekbones meant nothing to her. She was used to the unique quality of her beauty, and in her opinion it was not an advantage. Her experiences had convinced her that a beautiful woman was just a pawn in a man's world, rarely taken seriously, and often abused. Beauty had killed both her mother and her sister, and she had no intention of falling into the same trap.

But that didn't mean she didn't want to fulfil herself as a woman. Just because she despised men, and all they stood for, she was not above using one to create her own destiny. She wanted a home, and a family, and after seven years of working to attain her ends she was now within sight of achieving them. So, why was she feeling so uncertain? She didn't regret what she had done, did she?

Turning the key, she fired the ignition, and after checking her mirror pulled out into the desultory traffic of Victoria Road. It was too late to go back to the university before lunch, and instead of driving into the city she headed west, towards Sullem Banks, and the river.

It was one of her favourite places, in the little north country town. Here the River Swan was flanked by long sloping stretches of turf, and it was possible to drive down and park on the river bank. When Beth first came to live in Sullem Cross, she had used to come here to escape the confines of her lonely bedsitter, and even now that she had a comfortable home of her own she still came here when she wanted to think.

But today her growling stomach drove her to seek some form of sustenance before she reached the Banks. A baker's, which served take-away sandwiches and polystyrene cups filled with coffee or tea, provided the necessary nourishment, and after finding a suitable spot Beth opened the pack of cheese and tomato toasties.

Munching on the sandwich, she watched a family of ducks making their way along the river bank. It was a popular haunt for families, and the ducks were no doubt hoping to attract a scattering of breadcrumbs, and, although Beth could have eaten both sandwiches and more besides, she yielded to the temptation to offer them a share. Besides, it was delightful to watch the ducklings scrambling over one another in their haste to reach a particular crumb, and her lips tilted at their obvious rivalry.

It also reminded her, if any reminder was necessary, of the confirmation she had received that morning, and her hand probed her still flat stomach, as if doubting the veracity of what she knew to be true. She was going to have a baby; her baby; no one else's.

But once again she felt that hollow feeling inside her. It wasn't *just* her baby, a small voice reminded her. It was just as much Alex Thorpe's as hers, and, even though he didn't know about it, it didn't alter that one inescapable fact.

But what of it? she defended herself. It wasn't as if she was depriving him of anything he wanted. Good heavens, he didn't even know of its existence, and even if he did she doubted he'd be overjoyed at the news. It would be a burden, an unwelcome burden, on a man who evidently didn't welcome responsibility. He had to have been in his late thirties, and by his own admission unmarried. Though, with hindsight, she had to admit, he had told her precious little about himself.

But then, she had been so busy avoiding telling him anything about herself, it hadn't seemed a disadvantage. On the contrary, everything about him had fitted her image of the man who was to father her child, and, while he could be a pimp or a drug-pusher, she didn't think he was.

She had known the risk she was taking long before she gatecrashed the party. In this time of AIDS, and other sexually-transmitted diseases, it wasn't wise to sleep with just anyone. That was why she had chosen Alex. Because he had looked strong and healthy; and reasonably safe.

Of course, she had also wanted a man whom she could seduce. Which in itself was a daunting prospect, considering she had never seduced a man before. But he had looked older than the other men at the party, and he had behaved like a man who was attracted to women. And, when he'd offered to buy her supper, she couldn't believe her luck.

Of course, taking him to the apartment had been a gamble. And plying him with Chivas Regal might have engineered her own downfall, or so she had read. Too much, and he might not have been able to do her bidding, however much he might have wanted to. Too little, and he might have turned her down.

But, in the event, Alex had proved himself more than equal to her expectations. Which was one of the reasons why she was suffering these pangs of—what? Conscience? Remorse? Guilt? She shivered. In all her calculations, she had never expected to enjoy it, and the fact that he had made her do so had left her with a distinct feeling of regret.

It hadn't been meant to be that way. Her intention had simply been to entice him into bed, and encourage him to violate her body. She hadn't expected him to be so—so patient. Or that he would realise she had never been with a man before. She gave a mirthless laugh. She had proved to be some *femme fatale*, she thought ruefully. She hadn't even known what to expect.

She blamed her inexperience, of course. All her life, she had kept men at arm's length, never letting any of them breach the protective shell she had built around herself. Friends she had made had all learned to respect her privacy, and if some of them thought she was weird it was not something that troubled her overmuch.

It was only now she was having to come to terms with the fact that knowledge gleaned from books could only ever be superficial. Her lack of experience had left her hopelessly ignorant of the workings of a man's body. Men weren't like animals. They didn't just mate, and walk away. More than that, they apparently had the capacity to prolong their enjoyment, and, totally without her volition, she had found herself sharing his need.

God!

She tossed the remainder of the sandwich out of the window, watching the antics of the ducklings with rather less enthusiasm now. How had it happened? How had a man she had met less than two hours before been able to cause such a fever in her body? Nothing remotely like it had ever happened to her before. Yet from the minute he'd entered the apartment, she'd had the uneasy feeling she was in over her head.

She should have called it a day there and then. It wasn't as if he hadn't given her the opportunity. On the contrary, without the liberal dose of alcohol, she doubted he'd have succumbed to her less than erotic charms. But, having gone so far, she had been unwilling to back off. She'd known she might never get up the courage to do such a thing again.

And, to all intents and purposes, she had been totally successful. Whatever the rights or wrongs of it might be, she had achieved her objective. She had had sex with a man she never intended to see again, a man who couldn't trace her. She was free and clear and pregnant, just as she'd wanted. And the sooner she stopped thinking about Alex Thorpe the better.

But it was easier said than done. Once again, as it had done numerous times over the last eight weeks, her mind shifted to wondering what had happened after she ran out on him. It was natural that she should be curious, she told herself. He was not the kind of man to take it lightly.

At first, she had gone over her own efforts to erase all trace of her identity, constantly worrying over every small detail she remembered, afraid that she might not have thought of everything. But her plan then, and now, seemed foolproof. The apartment she had used in London had been rented in an assumed name. The same name had been used to rent the small Peugeot, and her appearance at the party had been brief and anonymous. She had only learned of the party by chance. She had heard Tony, one of the students, bewailing the fact that he wouldn't be able to attend. Christina Lennox just happened to be his cousin's girlfriend, but there was no reason to connect Tony Thiarchos with the uninvited guest. To connect him with Elizabeth Ryan, she amended pedantically, wondering if she had been a little rash in using her own first name. But no. There must be several thousand Elizabeths in London alone, and ever since she left home she had always referred to herself as Beth— Beth Haley.

But, even after she had assured herself no one could trace her, she still hadn't been able to get Alex Thorpe out of her mind. She found he had left an indelible impression, and she hoped, now that she had achieved her ambitions, that what had happened would lose its importance.

She ought to be relieved that she had covered her tracks so completely. There seemed no way anyone could link a university lecturer from a small northern town with the kind of woman who'd pick up a man at a party in London. She doubted even her students would have recognised her behaviour—even if her appearance had been impossible to disguise.

So, all that remained was for her to complete the present term. She had already prepared the way for her absence. A year's sabbatical, ostensibly to write the book about eighteenth-century literature she had been planning, and then back to work the following year, when the baby was old enough to be left with a minder. She expected his—or her—appearance would cause some speculation. At twenty-nine, Miss—she never fudged the issue by calling herself Ms—Haley was regarded as something of an eccentric. She had never had a regular boyfriend, even though certain of her fellow lecturers had endeavoured to share her confidence. But, although she was known to be efficient at work, and popular with the students, she was essentially a private person. There would be questions, but she could handle them. One of the advantages of being reserved was that it discouraged a lot of prying.

Remembering she hadn't yet had a drink, she peeled off the plastic lid and brought the cup of coffee to her lips. The smell almost overpowered her, and, wishing she had just bought a fruit juice instead, she poured the lukewarm liquid out of the window. The ducks came to see what she was doing, but retired in disgust when they found the coffee had already seeped into the ground. 'Well, you did have most of the sandwich,' she informed them drily, smiling at her own foolishness, and, turning the key, she started the car.

She was leaving the English building later that afternoon, when one of her fellow professors hailed her. 'Beth!' called Nigel Dorner, hurrying across the quad-rangle to intercept her. 'I'm so glad I've caught you. I'm having a little reception tomorrow night, in the Students' Union, and I wondered if you'd care to come. It's an informal gathering, pre-finals and all that. A chance for the staff and students to get together before exams and degrees take precedence. What do you think?'

Beth folded her arms around the pile of papers she was carrying, and waited until he had reached her. Nigel was in his forties, and although he made a big thing about his sporting activities he was decidedly over-weight. He was panting by the time he came up beside her, and she allowed him to get his breath back before saying, 'I don't think so, Nigel. I've got these papers to read, and I promised David I'd take his Thursday evening seminar. I'll have to do some preparation——'

'Oh, Beth!' Nigel expelled his breath on a disappointed sigh, and ran a hand over his thinning hair. 'I was sure you'd come. It is almost the end of term. Surely you can take one evening off to have a little fun?'

Beth caught her lower lip between her teeth, wondering why Nigel persisted in thinking she needed to have some fun. Ever since she had made it known she wasn't interested in having a relationship with any of the younger members of the faculty, Nigel Dorner, who was a divorcee, and Andrew Holroyd, who was slightly older than Nigel and a bachelor, had been vying for her company. It was as if they didn't believe she could live without a man's attentions, and they had evidently decided she'd prefer an older man.

'Look, Nigel,' she said, not wanting to hurt his feelings, 'college get-togethers aren't really my thing. I only attend when it's absolutely necessary, and I do have a lot of work I want to finish before the holidays.'

Nigel hunched his shoulders. They were broad shoulders, she noticed, unwillingly finding herself comparing them to Alex Thorpe's. It was because he had been so much on her mind today, she thought irritably, but she couldn't help conceding that that was where the likeness ended. As well as having broad shoulders, Alex had also been tall, whereas Nigel was little more than her own height of five feet eight. And tubby, into the bargain, she added, his bulging belly always reminding her of Mr Pickwick.

She supposed Andrew Holroyd was the better looking of the two, and he was taller, and less weighty. But neither of them attracted her in the slightest.

'Well, I worry about you, Beth,' Nigel said now, turning to an approach that had proved successful in the past. Whenever anyone said they were worried about her, Beth usually gave in. Not least because she disliked the thought that her behaviour was a cause for concern. 'You live alone in that old house, with only the ghosts for company, and if it weren't for your work here I doubt you'd have any social life.'

Beth stiffened. 'I really don't think that's any concern of yours, Nigel,' she said coldly. 'How I choose to spend my time is my affair——'

'Of course it is.' Nigel realised he had gone too far this time and hurriedly retrenched. 'And I know it's not for want of an alternative. Good heavens, you could be out every night if you wanted to. I know that. But you know what they say about—about all work and no play.'

He looked so discomfited now, Beth took pity on him. It wasn't Nigel's fault that she had such a poor opinion of his sex, and once she left the faculty, albeit temporarily, she would be cut off from her normal round of acquaintances.

Taking a breath, she allowed a smile to lift her lips for a moment, and then said, 'All right. What time does this get-together start?'

Nigel couldn't believe his luck. 'Oh—um—half-past eight,' he offered, almost dropping the books he was carrying in his haste to show his enthusiasm. 'I say, will you come? I'd be awfully flattered.'

'Not too flattered, I hope,' murmured Beth drily, starting towards the car park. 'Until tomorrow, then.'

'Until tomorrow,' echoed Nigel eagerly. 'Would you like me to—to pick you up?'

'Oh, I think I can find my own way to the Students' Union,' Beth assured him lightly. 'Goodbye. I'll see you tomorrow.'

She was aware of him watching her as she strode to where the Renault was waiting, and she wondered if she had made a mistake by accepting his invitation. She wouldn't like him to get the wrong idea, not with the summer break looming. As far as she knew, Nigel was staying on campus, and it could prove difficult if he started to get the wrong idea.

Still, she consoled herself, unloading her burden of essays on to the back seat, she could always deal with that contingency if it arose. For the present, she had quite enough to think about, not least what she was going to wear tomorrow evening.

Her house, the house she had bought four years ago, and which had considerably increased in value since that time, stood in a row of similar Victorian houses, over-looking Albert Square. The cul-de-sac was called Albert Terrace, and had evidently been named with the then Prince Consort in mind. During the past four years, Beth had steadily improved its appearance, and without losing its character at all she had had new wiring, and an adequate heating system installed. She knew it was too big for one person, but she had never intended to live there alone. And if the ghosts Nigel had taunted her with were sometimes more real than he imagined, they were not ghosts that Albert Terrace knew anything about.

The phone was ringing as she entered the long narrow hall that ran from front to back of the building, and she frowned. She had hoped to be free of complications for the rest of the evening, and she nudged the door closed with her foot, before picking up the receiver.

'Beth!'

It was Justine Sawyer, wife of one of the maths lecturers, and the closest thing she had to a friend on campus. Justine was the one person Beth still had to deal with in her calculations. In her early thirties, and a social worker, Justine had been married to Mike for more than ten years, without having a family. Justine didn't want children. She didn't like them, and she had begun to assume that Beth felt the same. How she would react to the news she had to deliver, Beth didn't know. Right now, she didn't even want to think about it.

'Hi, Justine.' Beth wedged her pile of papers on to the hall table, as she responded to the call, absently scanning the letters her cleaner, Mrs Lamb, had left there for her. 'You just caught me. I've just come in the door.'

'Yes, I gathered that. I was beginning to think one of the students had delayed you,' remarked Justine tersely. 'You have heard the news, I suppose. It's terrible, isn't it? He was such a pleasant boy.'

Beth frowned, putting the bills that had been distracting her aside. 'What boy, Justine?' she exclaimed.

'What are you talking about? Nigel intercepted me as I was leaving the English building. That's why I'm late. He wanted to ask me to some reception he's having tomorrow evening.'

'Well, there may not be a reception now,' declared Justine, sounding a little impatient. 'Beth, Tony Thiarchos is dead. Mike thinks he may have committed suicide.'

'Oh, no!'

Beth suddenly found she was a little weak at the knees. Groping for the banister, she lowered herself on to the second stair and took a steadying breath. It wasn't that she had known Tony Thiarchos very well. He wasn't even one of her students. But his girlfriend was, and that was how she'd got to know him. How she'd heard about the party in London.

'I thought you'd be upset,' said Justine, sounding slightly mollified now. 'His girlfriend—what was her name? Linda something-or-other—is one of your third years, isn't she?'

'Mmm.'

Beth was finding it very difficult to respond at all. It was always a tragedy when a young person was killed, and Tony Thiarchos had seemed to have everything to live for. He was young, good-looking, popular with his contemporaries. She couldn't believe he was dead. Much less that he had deliberately taken his own life.

'Mike thinks he was worried about his finals,' went on Justine. 'He said he thought there was a lot of pressure on him from his family to do well. They're going to be pretty shattered when they hear the news. I wonder if they'll try to keep it out of the papers?'

Beth blinked, struggling to escape from the sudden cloud that seemed to have engulfed her. She was letting herself get too involved, she thought. Tony Thiarchos had meant nothing to her. Just because she had used something he said in passing for her own ends was no reason to feel any sense of guilt now.

'I—why would they?' she managed, gripping the stair carpet beside her with tense fingers, and Justine gave a short laugh.

'Well, if they can't, no one can,' she retorted grimly. 'He's a Thiarchos, Beth. Surely even you've heard of Constantine Thiarchos! As in oil—and shipping, and God knows what else!'

Beth pulled herself together. 'I—didn't think,' she mumbled, not altogether truthfully. But she hadn't put the two names together. 'How—how did it happen?'

'His car hit a tree.'

Beth frowned. 'Well, why would you think——?'

'He was the only person in the car, Beth.' Justine was sounding impatient again. 'And it was broad daylight, for heaven's sake! He was a good driver. From what Mike says, he could handle that sports car of his like a professional.'

'Even so——'

'Oh, I know. It will probably be treated as an accident. These things usually are. But Mike saw what happened, and he doesn't——'

'Mike *saw* it!'

'Yes.' Justine sighed. 'It only happened an hour ago. Near Founder's Hall. That's why I thought—Beth, are you all right? You sound—well, funny.'

'I'm fine.' Beth was relieved to hear that her voice sounded almost normal. She tried to think coherently. 'So—what happens now?'

'Well, there'll have to be an inquest, of course. And his family will have to be informed. I believe his father lives in London. I imagine he'll be coming to arrange everything.'

Beth nodded. 'Poor Linda.'

'Yes. I expect it's pretty awful for her. They say they were really close. Not that his family would approve. People like the Thiarchoses don't marry girls like her.'

'Why?'

Beth tried to focus on the least horrifying aspect of the affair, and Justine made a scornful sound. 'Darling, we're too old to believe in all that romantic stuff. Let's face it, it was just a college infatuation. He'd have left this summer, and they'd have never seen one another again.'

Beth pushed herself somewhat wearily to her feet. 'I suppose you're right.'

'You know I am.' Justine sounded irritatingly smug. 'Now, how about you joining Mike and me for supper? I know it's short notice, but I think we could all use a little company tonight.'

Beth hesitated, but the thought of preparing a lonely meal for one had lost some of its appeal. She didn't want to be alone tonight. She didn't want to think about Tony Thiarchos. She didn't want to remember that without his grumbling about not being able to attend his cousin's birthday party she'd never have conceived the idea of gatecrashing the event. He'd been inadvertently responsible for her present condition; for her meeting Alex Thorpe—and that was something else she didn't want to think about...

CHAPTER TWO

ALEX'S fingers felt numb.

They shouldn't have felt numb, he thought irritably, wondering how he could feel so cold on such a warm day. It was absurdly warm for May in England. But the chill he was feeling came from deep within himself.

He wanted to put his hands in his pockets, but standing beside his son's grave with his hands in his pockets seemed disrespectful somehow. Not that Tony would have reproached him. His son had always been complaining about his father's concern for doing the right thing.

Well, he wasn't doing the right thing now, Alex thought bitterly, watching his son's casket being lowered into a grave in an English churchyard. Tony's grandfather had wanted—*had demanded*—that Alex bring Anthony's body back to Greece for burial. Constantine had wanted his grandson laid to rest beside his wife and his mother, but Alex had ignored him. It was a small thing, a small rebellion, but Tony would defeat his grandfather in death as he had never done in life.

Besides, there was the girl to deal with. Tony's wife, if that incredible scrap of paper was to be believed. Was she the reason his son had crashed his car? Because Tony had been afraid to tell his father and his grandfather he'd married without their consent?

Alex's jaw hardened. He couldn't believe that was so. It was too easy. Too simple a solution for something that surely had a deeper significance. But what? He had racked his brain trying to come up with an answer. He had hoped the girl could tell him. Linda. He tried out the name on his tongue. Linda Daniels—no, Linda *Thiarchos*. His lips twisted. His daughter-in-law!

The service was ending. Bending to scatter a handful of soil over the mahogany casket, Alex felt a crippling sense of pain. God, he wished he had someone he could turn to right at this moment. Even Lucia—though she was far away in South America, too wrapped up with her new life, and her new family, to spare the time to attend her eldest son's funeral.

Besides, it was a maudlin wish. He and Lucia had never had anything in common—except their son—and their marriage had ended, as it had begun, in acrimony. Something else he had to thank his father for, he thought wearily. And if he thought Constantine had had a hand in this...

He straightened and, as he did so, his eyes were riveted by the sight of a tall slim woman, standing behind, and to one side, of his son's wife. He blinked once, twice, and then shook his head, as if the tumult of his emotions had caused some blurring of his vision. But no. She was still there. Across the grave. Her hand resting lightly on the girl's shoulder, as if offering silent support.

He looked down at the ground, incapable of believing that she was actually there. That Elizabeth Ryan was standing at the other side of the grave. And now, conversely, he hoped she hadn't recognised him. It was obvious his name meant nothing to her. Alexander Thiarchos was a far cry from plain old Alex Thorpe.

But his fear that she might recognise him had nothing to do with who he was. On the contrary, in the past three months, he had used all the means at his disposal to try and find her. And that had meant employing the whole weight of the Thiarchos name to get a result. But it had been for nothing. As of this morning, he had been no nearer to discovering where she was or why she'd disappeared.

No, his fear now was that she might recognise him, and disappear again. And he wanted to know where she had been hiding. *Needed to know*, with an intensity that had bordered on the insane sometimes. It wasn't just that such a thing had never happened to him before—

though it hadn't. No, he was furious that she had treated him like a fool.

He chanced another glance in her direction, keeping his head lowered, looking at her through the dark veil of his lashes. Yes, that was Elizabeth Ryan all right, if indeed that was her name. Good God, after all the money he had spent on private investigators, that she should turn up at his son's funeral. Who the hell was she? What was she doing here?

The ironic thing was, he'd never once thought of calling his son and asking him if he knew her. It would have been difficult anyway, and it hadn't occurred to him that Tony might know who she was. Perhaps he hadn't. Perhaps she was just a friend of Linda's. After all, both Nick and Christina had denied they'd ever invited her to the party.

'Mr Thiarchos...'

The priest was at his shoulder, offering him his condolences, and Alex was obliged to lift his head to give his thanks. But he turned, so that the priest stood between him and the two women, as he exchanged a few words with the mourners, before they all trooped to their cars.

His brother, George, was there, of course, with his wife, Simone, and their two sons, Nick and George Junior. There were uncles and aunts, a whole army of cousins, and numerous other relatives and friends, who regarded any ceremony, happy or sad, as a reason for getting together.

Only his father was absent. Ostensibly, Constantine was recovering from a cold, but Alex knew the old man had stayed away, in the hope that he would change his mind. But, in this, Alex had been determined to have his own way. Besides, if Tony did have a widow, he defended himself, it would be easier for her to visit his grave if it was here, in London.

He hunched his shoulders. What ought he to do now? In other circumstances, he would have been expected to join his daughter-in-law, and escort her back to the house. But these were not normal circumstances on two counts, and the one conversation he had had with the girl had not been a comfortable affair.

But what the hell? he thought tersely. How was he supposed to react to the news that his twenty-year-old son had been a married man for almost six months? Tony had been wrong. He should have told him. And now Tony was dead, with no chance of conciliation on either side.

Squaring his shoulders, preparing himself to face not only his new daughter-in-law, but also the woman who had haunted his dreams for the past ten weeks, he turned round—and then felt a dizzying sense of disorientation. They'd gone. Linda, and Elizabeth Ryan. While he had been observing the proprieties, they had both disappeared. Lord, he thought, as his stomach hollowed, was he going mad?

'Something wrong, Uncle Alex?'

It was Nick, and Alex gazed at his nephew with blank unseeing eyes. For a moment, it was beyond his capabilities to get any words past his lips, but then the world around him steadied, and he expelled a nervous breath.

'I—Linda—she appears to have gone,' he said, hoping he didn't sound as desperate as he felt, and Nick nodded.

'I noticed.'

'You noticed?' Alex repeated his words harshly, and then, getting himself under control again said, 'So, perhaps you noticed where they—where she went. I need to speak with her.'

Nick frowned, pushing his hands into the pockets of his dark suit. 'Is that wise?' he asked doubtfully. 'Perhaps you should just let her come to you, if she wants to.' He paused. 'Dad thinks you've been more than generous letting her come here.'

'Does he?' Alex was curt. He didn't much care what George thought. The fact was, his brother found it a damn sight easier being tough with a woman than he ever did with a man. 'Well, if you've heard that she and I exchanged a few words at the college a week ago, forget it. We both said a lot of things we probably shouldn't have. And, if she is Tony's wife—widow——'

'Dad says the marriage certificate is authentic.'

'—then I guess I have to find out what she intends to do, don't I?'

Nick nodded again. 'I guess so.'

'And—whether she had any idea what Tony——'

Nick shrugged. 'Do you think she'd tell you? Even if she knew?'

'She has to talk to someone,' said Alex flatly, as the image of a slim, startlingly beautiful woman, with silvery blonde hair, flashed across his mind. 'Come on, Nico, do you know where she's gone or don't you?'

'They might know,' answered Nick obliquely, gesturing towards a group of young people who were just dispersing from the graveside. 'They're students—from the university. They all came down from Yorkshire this morning.'

Alex brought the Mercedes to a halt at the kerb, but although he switched off the engine he didn't immediately get out of the car. He was tired, he thought wearily, gazing at the lace-curtained windows of the small semi. Bone-tired, and in no mood to conduct any kind of interview. But it had to be done. From what he could gather, Linda was planning on going back to the university in a couple of days. To take her exams, if the students he had spoken to could be believed. How she could think of taking exams in the present circumstances was beyond his comprehension. But if that was what she intended to do, the sooner he spoke to her the better, before time, and his resentment, got in the way.

Not that that was the only reason he had come here tonight, he conceded, hunching his shoulders against an unwilling tide of emotion. He hadn't left his brother to make his excuses to the rest of the family just because he needed to speak to his daughter-in-law. It was the woman who had accompanied her he needed to see.

Forgive me, Tony, he prayed, but his confrontation with Elizabeth Ryan was long overdue.

He glanced at his watch. It was nearly half-past six, but he was surprised to find it was still so early. A whole lifetime seemed to have passed since he'd seen her in the churchyard earlier that afternoon. Since then, he had had only one objective. To see her, and tell her what he thought of her.

He knew his family and friends, his business acquaintances, and the members of his household staff, all thought grief was responsible for the unnatural air of optimism he had adopted throughout the reception that had followed the burial. And perhaps it was. Conversely, during the past week, he had thought of little else but Tony, and the guilt he felt at not being there when his son might have needed him most. He had gone around in a daze, hardly aware of what he was doing. All through the police enquiries, and the inquest that followed, he had felt as if he was living some awful nightmare. Only when he'd spoken to Linda had he let his feelings show.

But now his mind felt active again. Ever since he'd seen Elizabeth Ryan in the churchyard, it had had a new focus. For a period, at least, he could use his anger towards her to blot out the pain of his son's death. Thinking of her could keep him sane; give his mind time to heal.

Pulling the keys out of the ignition, he thrust open his door and got out of the car. He was still wearing the dark suit and black tie he had worn to the funeral, and his sombre clothes stood out in the quiet street, where most men were in their shirt-sleeves. The warm day had given way to an even warmer evening, and the usual activities of trimming hedges and mowing lawns were much in evidence here.

But not at Number Seventeen, he noticed, locking the car, and approaching the gate. Apart from an upstairs window being open, and a curtain billowing in the gap, the house looked deserted. They were probably all in the back, he decided. Linda, her parents, and—Elizabeth Ryan.

There was no bell, so he knocked on the panels, which were interleaved with strips of fluted glass. An encouragement for thieves, he thought, imagining how easy it would be to break the glass and unlock the door. Would he go that far, if they refused to speak to him?

Deciding his mind was wandering again, he rested one hand against the wall beside the door and knocked again. He should have let Spiro come with him, as George had wanted him to do, he thought. His burly chauffeur could be relied upon to handle most situations. It was only because he hadn't wanted to intimidate the girl that he had insisted on coming here alone.

At last, when he was seriously considering all alternatives, he heard someone coming along the hall to the door. He could see a shadow through the glass panels, and his stomach clenched in sudden anticipation. What if it was Elizabeth Ryan? he thought, aware that he was not as in control as he'd imagined. God, why did the woman do this to him? He was as apprehensive now as he had been on his first date.

A key turned, the door opened—and his daughter-in-law was standing there, looking at him. 'Why—Mr Thiarchos!' she exclaimed, briefly too shocked to show any hostility. And then, less hospitably, 'What do you want?'

She had been crying, Alex noticed. Her eyes were red, the lids white and puffy. In normal circumstances, he supposed she was a pretty girl. Attractive, anyway, with her wide, mobile mouth, and short brown curly hair. She wasn't tall, and she was inclined to carry a little weight, but in something other than an oversized T-shirt and worn jeans he guessed she could look quite presentable.

'I—we need to talk,' Alex replied at last, looking beyond her into the narrow hall of the house. 'May I come in?'

Her breath escaped in a rush. 'Why?'

'Because I'd prefer not to discuss my private affairs on the doorstep,' declared Alex evenly, and she raised a protesting hand.

'No, I don't mean that. I mean—why do you want to talk to me? I—I don't think we have anything to say to one another.'

'Don't you?' Alex endeavoured to hold on to his patience. He had to remember that this had to have been almost as hard for her as it had been for him, and he couldn't rush her. 'Well, trust me, we do.'

Linda sniffed. 'If you've come here to tell me I needn't expect any help from the Thiarchos family, then save your breath. I don't want anything from you——'

'I haven't.' Alex straightened. 'Look—I know it hasn't been easy for you. And—and I haven't made it any easier; I know that, too. But you have to cut me a little slack here. We all say things we don't mean sometimes. I know I do, and I guess you do, too.'

Linda gave him a suspicious look. 'So, you haven't come to cause trouble?'

Alex shook his head. 'No.'

She hesitated a moment longer, and then she moved to one side so that he could step into the hall. It was a silent invitation, but Alex took it, taking the door from her unresisting fingers and closing it behind him.

'You'd better come through,' said Linda, leading the way along the hall. 'I'll introduce you to Kathie.'

Kathie? Alex frowned. Who the hell was Kathie? Not her mother, obviously. Her sister, perhaps? Or the woman he knew as Elizabeth Ryan? His nerves tightened.

Deciding he'd find out soon enough, he said nothing as he followed her into a small conservatory at the back of the house. The light in the glass-walled extension was dazzling, and the heat was such that Alex wouldn't have been surprised to see grapes ripening on the vines that curled up from a variety of pots and containers. But his attention was caught by the sight of a woman, sitting in a cane chair beneath the windows, and it wasn't until she got up and came towards them that he saw that her silvery hair was grey and not blonde.

'This is my foster mother, Kathie Adams,' said Linda, with some reluctance. 'Kathie, this is Tony's father.'

'Tony's—father?' The woman looked at Alex with evident surprise. 'I—how do you do, Mr Thiarchos? I'm sorry to meet you in such unhappy circumstances.'

'Yes.' Alex took the hand she proffered with controlled politeness. 'I'm sorry, too. And I hope you'll forgive me for coming here unannounced.'

'Why, of course.' Mrs Adams was as sociable as his daughter-in-law was reserved. 'Won't you sit down, Mr Thiarchos? Let me get you something to drink. Tea, perhaps?'

Alex, who had been hoping for something a little more substantial, managed a slight smile. 'Tea sounds fine,' he conceded, waiting until Linda had perched herself on the edge of the wide window-seat before taking the chair the older woman had offered. 'Thank you.'

'Good.' Mrs Adams gave her foster daughter an encouraging look. 'Well, I'll leave you two to have a chat, hmm? I won't be long, Linda.'

Linda flashed her a grateful look, though Alex had the impression that she would rather have made the tea herself. Still, she remained where she was, gripping the sill at either side of her jeans-clad knees with nervous hands. For the first time since he had learned his son had a wife, Alex felt a trace of sympathy for her. Dear God, what an end to their married life! And he'd thought his divorce from Lucia had been ugly.

'So,' he said, realising it was up to him to say something, 'why did you rush away after the funeral? You should have come back to the house.' *Both of you.*

'Your house?' Linda gave him a sceptical look. 'Oh, yes. I'm sure I'd have been welcome there.'

Alex spread his legs, resting his arms along his thighs, and looked down at the tiled floor beneath his feet. 'All right,' he said. 'Perhaps I deserved that. Perhaps I wasn't as understanding as I should have been when I——'

'You were damned rude!' she retorted, a break in her voice. 'You came up to Yorkshire looking for a scapegoat, and I was there!' She pulled a tissue out of her pocket and scrubbed at her nose. 'How do you think I felt?'

'Yes.' Alex lifted his head. 'Yes—well, perhaps that's so. But you know what they were saying, what they're still saying, if it comes to that. That Tony drove into that tree deliberately——' He broke off as the whole horror of the situation washed over him again. 'I'm sorry. I'm doing this badly. You'll have to forgive me. What I want to say is—did you have any inkling that he might——?' He shook his head. 'My God, he was due to leave in a few weeks. I thought he was happy!'

Linda bent her head. 'When you thought about him at all,' she muttered, scuffing her feet, and Alex gazed at her with sudden anger.

'What's that supposed to mean?'

'Well . . .' Linda swallowed, and he guessed she had bitten off more than she could chew. 'How—how often have you seen him in the past year? How many times have you been up to Sullem Cross?'

Alex tamped down his resentment, but he wasn't used to having his actions questioned. By anyone. 'I—saw him a couple of times——'

'In London.'

'So? I have a business to run, Linda. Tony understood that.'

'Did he?'

'I thought he did.' Alex's cheek muscles ached with the effort of controlling his emotions. 'I gave him everything he wanted. A decent place to live; clothes; a car!'

'Presents,' said Linda contemptuously. 'You gave him presents. You treated him like a child. He never had any money of his own.'

'He had access to funds.'

'Credit cards,' she retorted. 'You didn't know your son very well, Mr Thiarchos. Tony couldn't live on what you gave him.'

Alex's fists clenched. 'You mean he couldn't support a wife on what I gave him,' he countered. 'No, I'll give you that.'

'I didn't want his money!' Her voice was shrill. 'I didn't take any of it!'

'No?'

'No.'

They were both on their feet now, facing one another, and the sound of the outer door slamming didn't immediately register in Alex's tired brain. He was too intent on finding out the truth about his son. He had even forgotten the other reason he had come here.

'And you expect me to believe that?' he was demanding harshly, when someone appeared in the doorway to the conservatory.

'For heaven's sake, Linda, what's going on here?' the newcomer exclaimed. 'Dear Lord, can't this wait? Tony was only buried this afternoon!'

Alex's first thought was that her voice was the same, smooth and husky, soothing his jagged senses with a fine stroke of velvet. Then his world tilted. God, it was her, he saw unsteadily. The same, yet not the same. The same height and colouring; the same exotic beauty, but softer, somehow, gentler. She had a little more flesh on her bones than he remembered. And her hair was definitely longer than before. It brushed her shoulders now, thick and silky, its weight removing its tendency to curl.

She hadn't seen him yet, hadn't identified him as anything more than Tony's father. Her attention was all on his daughter-in-law, and he was able to look at her unobserved. He suddenly wished he had chosen some other way to do this. But he hadn't expected his own irrational sympathy for her, and what had seemed so simple back at the house was now intensely complicated. Complicated by the fact that he suddenly had the urge to bury his face in the pale beauty of her hair, he thought disgustedly. He was unutterably relieved when Linda broke the spell.

'It's all right, Beth.' *Beth*? So it was Elizabeth, then. 'Mr Thiarchos was just leaving, weren't you, Mr Thiarchos?'

Was he? Alex hauled his unruly senses back into line, and endeavoured to adopt a neutral expression. But he noticed that Linda was making no attempt to introduce them, and that angered him, too.

'Won't your—Mrs Adams—think it strange if I do?' he suggested politely, and had the doubtful privilege of watching Elizabeth's composure disintegrate. She looked at him properly for the first time, and he met her horrified gaze with carefully dispassionate eyes. Then, deliberately, he held out his hand. 'Hello. I'm Alex Thiarchos. And you must be—Miss——?'

'Haley,' she got out hurriedly, and his eyebrows arched in knowing acknowledgement.

'Haley,' he agreed, not allowing her to look away. 'Were you a friend of my son's, too?'

Beth moistened her lips, triggering memories of that night, memories Alex would sooner forget, and lifted her shoulders in a curiously defeated gesture. 'Perhaps,' she said, and he realised she was having some difficulty in actually saying anything.

But once again Linda intervened. 'Miss Haley is a lecturer, from the university,' she told him brusquely. 'She very kindly agreed to come with me. Not just—not just as a representative of the university, but—but as—my friend.'

CHAPTER THREE

BETH remembered a comedy show that used to be on television, where one of the characters was always saying, 'Don't panic! Don't panic!' She felt like that character now, and, no matter how she fought the emotion, panic was all she could feel.

Dear God, she fretted, she should have realised the chance she was taking by coming here. When Linda had needed a friend, she should have let someone else take the part. She had known there might be people who had attended the party at Tony's funeral. But she had foolishly imagined that no one would recognise her—not on such an occasion.

And she had felt so sorry for Linda, so desperate to do something—*anything*—to make amends. No matter how she'd tried, she hadn't been able to detach herself from the tragedy, and by supporting Linda she'd hoped to make some reparation for what she'd done.

And she'd succeeded. Or so she'd believed. Attending the funeral with Linda had been no problem at all. It had been a very moving occasion, and, as Linda had assured her she had no intention of going back to the Thiarchos residence afterwards, any awkward confrontations had been avoided. But who could have anticipated that Alex Thorpe would turn up here, just when she had thought she was home free?

Only he wasn't Alex Thorpe, she acknowledged sickly. He was Alex *Thiarchos*! Tony's father. Son of Constantine Thiarchos, who everybody knew was one of the richest men in the world. Dear God! And she had picked him up and taken him home, as if he were some penniless drifter. She'd used him. She'd taken advantage of his semi-inebriated state, and seduced him. Lord, what would he do now?

'I guess I have to thank you, Miss Haley.'

She heard his words, but it was from a distance. The terracotta and cream tiles that stretched between them were wavering in and out of focus, and she knew, though she had never done such a thing before, that she was going to faint. *He had known*, she realised, as the buzzing in her ears drowned out the rest of what he was saying. He had expected to see her. She clutched the doorframe with hands that were suddenly sticky with sweat. She couldn't faint now, she thought wildly. She couldn't give him any suspicion that their night together had produced anything more than a bad hangover. Not now. Maybe not ever...

And then his arm was around her, supporting her, preventing her from slipping down on to those pretty tiles that suddenly seemed so attractive. In fact, the whole concept of losing consciousness was gaining appeal with every second, and she fought his will to rescue her with every nerve in her body.

But the trouble was, she was already feeling stronger. She wasn't one of those frail women who displayed their femininity by swooning at every emotional obstacle. In fact, until today, she had never even felt close to passing out, and she could only assume it was her condition that had aggravated her weakness. Her condition...

She lifted her hand, which was still inclined to shake a little, and endeavoured to free herself from his unwelcome embrace. But the muscles in the arm that still circled her waist were disturbingly strong, and although he loosened his hold he didn't let her go.

'Oh, Beth!' It was Linda who spoke first. 'Are you all right? We thought you were going to faint. You look awfully pale. Hadn't you better sit down?'

'Not in here,' said Alex Thiarchos flatly, and both women looked at him, with differing measures of resentment. 'It's too hot,' he added, using his hold on Beth's waist to propel her into the cooler shadows of the hall. 'And if your mother's got any brandy, Linda, I suggest you get Miss Haley a drink.'

'I don't drink brandy,' protested Beth, but Linda was already brushing past them to do Alex's bidding.

'I'll see what's happening about the tea,' she said, nodding, apparently having forgotten that five minutes ago she had been telling him to leave. 'I won't be a minute, Beth. Go into the front room, and put your feet up.'

'I'm all right.'

As Linda disappeared through the door that led into the kitchen, Beth managed to detach herself from Alex Thiarchos's hold, and stepped back from him. In the narrow hallway, he was frighteningly big and aggressive, and, although he hadn't said anything—yet—to upset her, the way he was looking at her promised retribution.

'How did you know?' she whispered fiercely, as soon as the kitchen door closed behind Linda, and she saw his dark brows descend.

'Know what?' he asked politely, but she knew instinctively that he was playing with her.

Like a cat with a mouse, she thought, disliking the analogy.

And not just any cat, but a rather large predator—playing with a decidedly insignificant mouse.

'How did you know who I was?' she repeated, in the same sibilant tone. And then, realising that either Linda or her foster mother could emerge from the kitchen at any moment and find them there, she felt around behind her for the door into the parlour.

'I didn't,' he responded, moving towards her, and she sucked in her breath in alarm. But all he did was lean past her and turn the handle she had been searching so inadequately to find.

Beth stepped back quickly, and away from the disturbing heat of his hard, muscled frame. 'You must have,' she got out jerkily, glancing behind her to make sure she was in no danger of tripping over. The last thing she wanted was for him to have to put his arms around her again. The experience had been too fraught, too un-settling. And much too painfully familiar.

'I didn't,' he assured her, allowing the door to close and resting back against it. 'Linda just introduced us.'

She didn't believe him, but his position successfully prevented any escape. Her only relief came from knowing that Linda and Mrs Adams would be back soon. And before they did she had to get herself under control.

She shook her head helplessly, running one hand under the weight of her hair and feeling the damp tendrils clinging to her neck. She couldn't believe his arrival here was a coincidence. And why hadn't she recognised him this afternoon, when he'd been standing only a few feet away?

The answer was obvious, of course. The possibility that the man she had picked up at the party and Tony's father being one and the same person had never even occurred to her. How could it? Tony had been twenty, going on twenty-one; he had been married, for heaven's sake! Alex Thiarchos didn't look old enough to have a son of Tony's age. And although she knew he must be forty, at least, he had the compelling masculinity of a much younger man.

It was the old adage that you saw what you expected to see. She had known that the dark-clad stranger she had glimpsed across the grave was Tony's father, so she had gifted him with what she thought was an appropriate age and appearance. His head had been bent most of the time anyway, and she had had to rely on her imagination. It wasn't her fault if she had pictured him with lined features and greying hair. Just as it wasn't his fault that this had happened.

She lifted her hands, linked her fingers together, and pressed them against her lips. 'I—don't know what to say.'

And she didn't. She was speechless; bereft of all rational thought. All she could think was that he was infinitely more attractive than she remembered, and that was something else she couldn't cope with.

'You could begin by telling me why you gave me a false name, a false address; and why you ran out on me?' he suggested, his tone low and carefully controlled. 'But not now. Not here. I don't think you'd like Linda or her mother to know how you behave in your spare time.'

'That's not—not how I—normally behave in my spare time,' Beth choked defensively. Good God, what did he think she was? He knew he had been the first man to... to...

'And I'm supposed to believe that, am I?'

He straightened away from the door, his broad shoulders flexing beneath the fine cloth of his suit. He was angry, she could see that now, and her nerves tightened at the thought of what he could do to her. And not just to her character, she thought anxiously. To her career...

'It's the truth!' she exclaimed, gazing at him imploringly. 'You have to believe me.'

His brows lifted in bitter scepticism, just as the door was propelled inwards behind him. He moved out of the way to let Mrs Adams, followed closely by Linda, come into the room, and they both stood in silence as the older woman set down the tray she was carrying on a low coffee-table.

'You should be sitting down, Beth,' Kathie Adams declared, gesturing towards the sofa, and, although what she most wanted to do was run, Beth complied. 'Here,' went on her hostess, handing her a glass, 'it's not brandy, it's whisky, but it's better than nothing. Don't you think so, Mr Thiarchos?'

Alex inclined his head. 'So long as—Miss Haley can swallow it,' he conceded, pushing his hands into the pockets of his suit jacket. 'I think she's feeling a bit better, aren't you, Miss Haley? It was very hot in the conservatory.'

Beth made a positive movement of her head, trying desperately to swallow the fiery liquid. But her uncertain stomach was rejecting it with equal determination, and when the tea was poured she surreptitiously substituted the cup for the glass.

Linda watched her for a few minutes, and then, as if assured that Beth hadn't suffered any ill effects from her near-faint, she turned to Alex. 'Thanks,' she said, and Beth knew what it must be costing her to thank this man for anything. 'For being there when you were needed,' Linda went on, lifting her shoulders in a reluctantly grateful gesture. 'But I think it might be best if you left now.'

'Linda!' That was Mrs Adams, ever the peace-maker, and Beth expelled her breath a little wearily as Linda's foster mother chided her daughter for behaving so outrageously. 'Mr Thiarchos is welcome to stay and have tea with us!' she exclaimed. 'Please sit down, Mr Thiarchos. I don't know what's come over Linda. She's not usually so impolite.'

Alex withdrew his hands from his pockets. 'Thank you,' he said, and Beth's spirits sank even lower, 'but I hope you'll forgive me if I decline your invitation, after all. It's obvious that this isn't the proper time to discuss what we have to discuss, and I suggest I come back at a more suitable moment.' He glanced at Beth. 'For all of us.'

Mrs Adams pressed her hands together. 'Well—if you're sure——'

'You heard him, Kathie,' declared Linda tersely. 'And perhaps you'd ring first,' she added, looking at Alex with cold defiance. 'Just in case we're busy. The number's in the book.'

Alex inclined his head, and as he did so a lock of his dark hair slid forward on to his forehead. His hair was very dark, Beth noticed unwillingly, and overlong at the back. But it suited him, thick and smooth and silky. And she knew from personal experience that it felt as clean as it looked.

She wondered suddenly if her baby would be dark, too. Like *him*. Like its father. It was strange to think that it would have Greek blood in its veins, as well as

English. Though just a quarter, she conceded, remembering Linda had told her that Tony's father was only
half-Greek.

And then the enormity of what had happened hit her.
Until now, she had been too busy fending off his questions to think of it, but suddenly the significance of her
circumstances swept over her. She wasn't just expecting
any baby. She was expecting Alex Thiarchos's baby. And
he had just lost his only son. What would he do if he
found out? Could he take her baby away from her?

He lifted his hand now, pushing long tanned fingers
through his hair, restoring it to its former position. The
action parted the two sides of his jacket, exposing a
wedge of grey silk. It also exposed buttons, strained by
his movements, and between the buttons taut flesh, and
a glimpse of body hair. That shadow of dark hair tormented her eyes, reminding her of things she wanted to
forget. She knew where that arrow of hair was leading,
where it thickened. She had to force herself to look away,
and not follow it to its source.

She might have to tell him, she fretted, her thoughts
returning to her earlier worries. How could she keep such
a thing from him, when obviously, at a time like this,
it could mean so much? He might resent her for what
she'd done. He might not even believe the child was his.
But some might say he deserved to be given the choice.
Could she live with such a secret?

She had to, she told herself fiercely, as his sombre gaze
met hers. She had worked so hard to make this happen.
She couldn't throw it all away, just because of a—a—a
what? An accident, she finished doggedly, refusing to
feel any remorse. It wasn't her fault she had mistaken
him for one of Nick's friends. It wasn't her fault that
Tony Thiarchos had died.

Linda was escorting him to the door now, and Beth
kept her eyes lowered. He was leaving, but she had no
doubt he would be back tomorrow. He was not the kind
of man to forget what happened. For some reason, he

resented what she'd done. And he wasn't going to forgive her.

'So what happened? Did you meet any of the Thiarchos family? What were they like?'

Justine poured herself another cup of coffee and joined Beth at the pine table. They were at the Sawyers' house, sitting in Justine's kitchen, sharing a mid-morning break, after spending an hour at the supermarket.

Beth shrugged, circling the top of her cup with an absent thumb. 'I—met—Alex Thiarchos, when he came to the house to see Linda,' she said at last, deciding there was no point in prevaricating about something that could easily be found out. 'He seemed—all right. I—didn't really have much to do with him.'

Justine arched her carefully plucked eyebrows, and gave her friend a curious look. 'Do I detect a note of caution? I gather you didn't like him?'

'I didn't say that.' Beth's denial was just a shade too vehement, and she hurriedly tempered it with a rueful smile. 'Really, I don't have an opinion about him,' she lied. 'But I don't envy Linda, having to deal with that family.'

'Why not?' Justine checked her knot of amber-coloured hair, and, apparently finding it satisfactory, idly played with the gold chain that circled her neck. 'I'd have thought she's damn lucky to have that marriage certificate. It must entitle her to some compensation, financial or otherwise.'

Beth bent her head. 'She says she doesn't want anything from them.'

'When did she say that?'

'Several times, actually. I think she means it. She loved Tony. Really loved him, I mean. But now he's dead—well, I think she's just trying to get on with her life.'

'How touching!' Justine grimaced. 'Well, I'll reserve judgement, if you don't mind. With all the gossip there's been since the boy died, she may decide they owe her more than a few kind words.'

Beth frowned. 'What gossip?'

'Haven't you heard?' Justine stared at her impatiently. 'Honestly, Beth, I sometimes think you go around with your eyes and ears closed. You've heard the rumours, surely? That Tony Thiarchos was on drugs when he ran the Porsche into a tree?'

'No!'

Beth gazed at her, aghast. She couldn't believe it. She wouldn't believe it. Linda had never given her any inkling that she and Tony had been having problems of that sort. And she had confided in Beth quite a lot. Not least, the anger she felt towards Tony's father for continuing to treat him like a child. Surely, she would have said something, if that had been on her conscience.

'Yes,' Justine contradicted her now, her eyes bright with malicious intent. 'Don't be naïve, Beth. You know drugs are freely available on campus. How some of the kids can afford them goodness knows, but they do. And for someone like Tony Thiarchos that wouldn't have been an obstacle.'

Her meaning was obvious, but Beth didn't want to think about it. She didn't want to think about Alex's grief, if such a thing should come to light, she admitted unwillingly. It must have been hard enough for him, facing the horror of knowing that it might not have been an accident. How much worse would it be if it was revealed that Tony had been high on heroin or cocaine at the time?

'It can't be true,' she burst out suddenly, remembering the autopsy. 'They'd have found out. When— when they did the post-mortem. The coroner returned a verdict of accidental death. There was no mention of any probable cause or complication.'

Justine just looked smug. 'Money closes a lot of mouths,' she remarked, crossing one slim leg over the other. 'In any case, Beth, what's it to you? You only went to the funeral with the girl because she asked you to. It's no skin off your nose if her husband was a junkie!'

Beth's lips tightened. She didn't like it when Justine adopted that supercilious attitude. 'I just don't think you should go around repeating stories that have no basis in fact,' she retorted edgily. 'For heaven's sake, don't you think they've suffered enough?'

'Who? His family?' Justine gave her an old-fashioned look. 'Come on, Beth. People like that don't suffer. It's probably their fault he turned to drugs in the first place.'

'You don't know he did,' protested Beth, wide-eyed. Then, realising she was getting too worked up about something that really had nothing to do with her, she determinedly changed the subject. 'Um—when did you say you and Mike were going away?'

Justine now looked as if she knew exactly why Beth had asked that question, but she evidently decided it wasn't worth pursuing. 'The second Thursday in July,' she supplied, good-humouredly. 'You must be getting old, Beth. I distinctly remember telling you that less than a week ago. We drive down to Southampton that day, and get the ferry the day after.'

'Of course.' Beth looked suitably chastened. 'You must be looking forward to it. How long did you say you expected to be away?'

'It's still three weeks,' replied Justine, pulling a face. 'I'd like to stay away longer, but Mike wants to spend some time researching that paper he's preparing on differential calculus.' She grimaced. 'Dull, dull, dull! But I don't suppose you'd agree. You're doing the same, aren't you?'

'Well—not differential calculus,' said Beth, managing to swallow a mouthful of coffee without gagging. But the smell was nearly her undoing, and, realising it would be hard to explain why she suddenly had such an aversion to a drink she had always enjoyed, she pushed back her chair and got to her feet. 'I'd better be going.'

'Oh, must you?' Justine frowned, tilting her head to look up at her. 'You know, you're looking awfully pale, Beth. Are you sure you're feeling OK? Don't let this business with Linda Daniels get you down. She's leaving at the end of this term, isn't she? Let her worry about the Thiarchoses. Personally, I think they'll make a financial settlement on her. It's the simplest way. Unless she's pregnant, of course.'

'Pregnant!' Beth caught her breath. That thought hadn't even occurred to her. 'Do you think she is?'

'Well, it's possible, isn't it? And if she is I'm sure they'll want access to it. After all, as you say, losing your only son must be pretty traumatic, even for someone like—what did you say his name was? Alex Thiarchos?'

Beth nodded, her mouth drying unpleasantly. 'Alex Thiarchos, yes,' she agreed, through tight lips, as the implications of what Justine had suggested ran wildly through her head. If Linda *were* pregnant, it would certainly take the pressure off her. Or would it? Wasn't the whole idea of her pregnancy getting more and more bizarre?

'Anyway, I think you ought to make some plans to go away yourself,' declared Justine firmly. 'You need a holiday. We all do. I'd ask you to come with Mike and me, but the trailer only sleeps two, and the sanitary arrangements are fairly basic——'

'Oh, really—no.'

The last thing Beth wanted was for Justine to start feeling responsible for her. She still hadn't told her that she was pregnant, and her only consolation came from knowing she was going to have at least three weeks to think of an explanation.

She had toyed with the idea of going away completely; of finding some place—in East Anglia perhaps— where she could rent a house or an apartment, and put down roots until the baby was born. Then she could even pretend she had adopted the baby; that it wasn't hers at all. She could invent some imaginary cousin, who had found herself in difficulties, and had been only too willing to shift the burden on to Beth's shoulders.

But that was the coward's way out, she knew. And, in other circumstances, she'd never have countenanced it. But knowing who her baby's father was had changed things, and she was afraid that if Justine questioned her too closely she might say something indiscreet. And if Linda should be pregnant, too...

'Well, you think about what I've said,' said Justine seriously, getting to her feet, and Beth realised that once again she had won a reprieve. Not only that, Justine was giving her the perfect opportunity to leave Sullem Cross, and she might be a fool not to take it.

To her surprise, Linda was waiting for her when she got back to her house in Albert Terrace. The girl was sitting on the low wall that surrounded the tiny front garden, watching anxiously for her return. Beth parked the Renault at the kerb, feeling a sickly fluttering in her stomach. She couldn't imagine why Linda might want to see her. Not here, anyway. And as their only real association, outside of college, had been through the Thiarchos family, she couldn't help feeling anxious.

It was three days since she'd seen Linda. Three days since Beth had made an excuse about work piling up, and returned to Sullem Cross alone. She had left the morning after Alex Thiarchos had appeared at Mrs Adams' house, and if he had returned the following day to see her he had been disappointed.

But Linda's appearance now was disturbing. What did she want? What *could* she want? Surely even Alex Thiarchos would not have been insensitive enough to ask for her address?

Linda got up from the wall as Beth got out of the car. She was wearing a sleeveless vest and skin-tight jeans, and if she was pregnant there was no sign of it. But that meant nothing, reflected Beth tautly, running a nervous hand over the barely perceptible thickening of her own waistline. She didn't look pregnant either—but she was.

'Oh, Beth!'

Linda's greeting was hardly reassuring, and Beth's nerves tightened like violin strings. What had Alex done? What had he said? For something told her that the apprehension she could see on Linda's face had not been self-induced.

'Linda!' she exclaimed now, coming round the car to meet her with what she hoped was a suitable expression of concern. 'Is something wrong? When did you get back?'

'This morning,' said Linda, answering her second question first. She sniffed ominously. 'Can we go inside?'

'What? Oh, yes. Yes, I suppose so.'

As a rule, Beth didn't invite students to her home. If she wanted to interview them, she used her office at the university, and seminars were usually held in one of the rooms in the English building. But this was an exceptional situation, she acknowledged, as she opened the gate and led the way into the house. Linda wouldn't have come here unless she had something important to say.

The house was hot and humid. Beth had locked all the doors and windows before she went out, and now she went straight down the hall and into the kitchen to open the back door.

'Tea?' she asked, after that was done, and a refreshing breeze was wafting the stuffiness away. She held up the kettle, and Linda, who had come to stand in the doorway, nodded indifferently.

'If you like.'

Beth caught her lower lip between her teeth, reflecting how their relationship had changed in a few short days. Ten days ago, Linda wouldn't have dreamed of speaking so dismissively to her.

She filled the kettle, set the teapot and cups on a tray, and then gestured towards the front of the house. 'Shall we go into the sitting-room? We'll be more comfortable in there. I'll come back when the kettle boils.'

'All right.'

Linda turned back on herself and, walking a few yards along the hall, she indicated the second door on her left. 'In here?'

'Yes.' Beth followed her into the pleasantly cool room she used most evenings. She pointed to a chintz-covered sofa. 'Take a seat.'

Linda did so, perching on the edge of the cushions, and although Beth would have preferred to stand she seated herself in the armchair opposite. It was important that she at least try and maintain a casual manner, and she managed a polite arching of her brows to indicate that she was ready to hear whatever it was that had brought the girl here.

'I expect you think I've got a nerve coming here,' said Linda at last, scrubbing the heels of her hands across her cheeks, and Beth wondered if that was good news or bad.

'I—not at all,' she demurred. 'If there's anything I can do——'

'He wants me to go to Greece with him,' burst out Linda abruptly, and after all the things she had been anticipating Beth felt an overwhelming sense of relief.

'He does,' she said, in a thready voice. And then, clearing her throat, 'I assume you mean—Tony's father.'

'Of course.' Linda sniffed again, and hunched her thin shoulders. 'Oh, Beth, he's insisting that I have to go and be introduced to all Tony's relatives. He expects me to meet Tony's grandfather. Constantine Thiarchos. Have you heard of him? He wants me to go and be—be vetted by a man Tony hated!' And she burst into tears.

Beth was speechless. For a moment, she just sat there, staring at Linda's shaking shoulders, and then, gathering herself together, she got up from her chair and went to comfort her.

'Aren't you exaggerating?' she exclaimed helplessly, putting a reassuring arm around her. 'Linda, Tony can't have hated his own grandfather!'

'He did. He hated him.' Linda turned towards her, and buried her face against Beth's shoulder. 'He drove Tony to do what he did. I'll never forgive him for that.'

Beth blinked. It was difficult to feel any conviction for what Linda was saying, but the girl was trembling so badly, she was forced to accept that she believed it anyway. But what did she mean? What was she accusing Tony's grandfather of?

'Look,' she said, trying to calm the girl down, 'I know how you feel. Tony's accident—the funeral—well, it's all been a lot for you to take. And I think you've done wonderfully well. You've handled yourself with dignity, and it's bound to have been a strain. And it's only natural that you should feel resentful——'

'No!' Linda lifted her head, smearing her hands across her tear-stained face. 'No, you don't understand. It's not the way you think. I'm not just looking for someone to blame. What happened—happened. I don't know if it was an accident or not. I may never know. But I do know that Constantine Thiarchos was always on Tony's back. He expected too much of him. And—and Tony couldn't take it.'

Beth frowned. 'But, Linda, he had you.'

'Not to begin with, he didn't. Tony and me—we've only known one another for about fifteen months.' She moaned. 'I wish I had known him before. Before—before those people got their claws into him.'

Beth was confused. 'But, Linda, they're his family!'

'What? Oh, no.' Linda's expression lightened for a moment. 'I don't mean the Thiarchoses.' Her momentary trace of humour disappeared again. 'I mean the people who were hounding him for money!'

Beth stared at her. 'Are you saying Tony owed someone some money?' she echoed disbelievingly. 'But, surely——'

'He shouldn't have been short of cash, right?' Linda finished for her, and Beth inclined her head. 'Well, he was. Oh, he had credit cards. He could buy anything he wanted with credit cards. But, unfortunately, the people he was dealing with didn't deal in plastic!'

Beth drew away to kneel on the carpet beside her. At last, she thought she was beginning to understand. And what was emerging didn't bear thinking about.

And Linda suddenly seemed to realise just who she was confiding this to. Dragging a tissue out of her pocket, she blew her nose and got to her feet. 'I've got to go.'

'Not yet.' Pressing down on the arm of her chair, Beth came up beside her. 'I think you'd better tell me who was hounding Tony for money.'

'It doesn't matter.'

'It does matter.' Beth took a steadying breath. 'I think we're talking drugs here, aren't we, Linda? You're telling me that Tony was an addict.'

'No!' Linda's indignation was convincing, but she could tell by Beth's expression that she wasn't making much headway. 'It's true,' she protested, wringing the tissue between her hands. 'I wouldn't have married an addict, Miss Haley. Honestly. You have to believe me.'

Beth noticed the switch to the more formal mode of address, but she didn't comment on it. She was more concerned with what she had learned, and what she, an unwilling participant in the tragedy, should do with the information.

'Please,' Linda implored her. 'I'm not lying, Miss Haley.' And then, as if reconsidering, 'Tony—Tony was on drugs once. But he kicked the habit. He did. Only by then it was too late.'

'Too late for what?' Beth was wary.

'For the money!' exclaimed Linda urgently. 'He'd borrowed money to—to pay for—for what he needed. But he couldn't keep up the repayments. Not on what his father sent him anyway.'

Beth looked doubtful. 'Linda——'

'It's true!' she insisted. 'I swear it. God, since I found out the trouble he was in, I've been giving him most of what I earned working part-time at the burger bar as well. But it wasn't enough. It was never enough.'

'So why didn't he contact his father?' Beth suggested quietly. 'I'm sure, if he had——'

'He couldn't do that.' Linda was vehement.

'Why not?'

'Because—because he couldn't.' She wrapped her arms about herself, and shivered. 'You don't know them, Miss Haley. You don't know what they're like. If they'd known Tony had ever—had ever—well, you know. They'd have made him leave the university, go back to Greece. He and I—we'd never have seen one another again.'

Beth's brows drew together. 'I thought you said his father lived in London.'

'He does.'

'Then——'

'His father doesn't control the family business. His grandfather does. And, believe me, he'd have made sure Tony suffered for what he'd done.'

'Tony said that.'

'Yes. But I know it's true.'

Beth hesitated. 'How? You haven't met his grandfather.'

'No, but I've seen the letters he's written to Tony.'

'He wrote in English?' Beth was sceptical.

'No, Greek,' said Linda sulkily. 'Tony translated them for me.' She sighed. 'They were horrible letters, Miss Haley. I know they were. Tony was always upset after one of them arrived.'

Beth bit her lip. 'Even so——'

'Even so nothing. You don't know what Tony was like. He wanted to please his family; he did. He just—couldn't take the pressure.'

Beth shook her head again, incapable at that moment of finding anything to say. There was obviously some truth in what Linda was saying, but so many inconsistencies as well. A good lawyer would tear her story to shreds, she thought ruefully. And perhaps Tony had known that, and that was why he'd——

She stopped herself there. She didn't want to think about it. She refused to think about it. It was nothing to do with her. She was just Linda's tutor. This conversation had nothing to do her involvement with Alex Thiarchos.

'I don't know what I'm going to do,' Linda whispered now, gazing at her with tear-filled eyes. 'Why can't they leave me alone? I just want to do my exams, and forget all about it.'

Beth sighed. 'Linda.' She hesitated. 'Linda, have you thought how—how Tony's father, and grandfather, must be feeling? They've lost Tony, too. And you were his wife. It's natural that they would want to know you.'

'Well, I don't want to know them.'

'But that's childish,' said Beth flatly. 'Linda, they may think—that is—you could be pregnant!'

'I'm not.'

Beth's heart fluttered. 'Are you sure?'

'Sure, I'm sure.' Linda brushed her eyes with the tissue. 'It's probably just as well. Then they'd really have had a hold on me, wouldn't they?'

Beth bent her head, unwilling to consider that thought. 'Nevertheless——'

'You didn't mind my coming here, did you?' Linda ventured suddenly. 'You didn't mind me talking to you? You see, I couldn't tell Kathie. She wouldn't have understood. And I've got no one else.'

'No...'

Beth's denial was reluctant, but evidently Linda was reassured enough to go on. 'I hoped I could rely on you—Beth,' she tendered, reverting to her previous form of address. 'I mean, you were there; at the funeral. And—and at Kathie's, when Tony's father came to see me. You met him. You saw what he was like. I'm not used to dealing with people like him, but—well, he was kind to you, wasn't he? Grabbing you, when you felt faint, and looking after you like that. He liked you. I know he did. And I know he'd listen to you. That's why I want you to talk to him. I know you could tell him—so much better than I could—exactly how I feel!'

CHAPTER FOUR

ALEX drove the final few miles to the university. It was a deliberate decision, born out of his desire not to repeat that other fateful journey of less than two weeks ago. Then, he had flown to the local airport, and had his pilot transport him the rest of the way by helicopter. Time had seemed of the essence, though, as it turned out, he had had all the time in the world.

Nevertheless, as he drove through the small town, crowded with summer visitors, and saw the university buildings, gleaming in the afternoon sunlight at the other side of the river, he still felt the same pang of apprehension. God, it didn't seem possible that Tony was dead. It hardly seemed any time since he was a boy, attending school in Athens.

He remembered so well his father's anger, when Tony had announced that he wanted to go to university in England. Although the old man's second wife, Alex's mother, had been an Englishwoman, Constantine had not encouraged either of his sons to break with tradition. Both George and Alex had married women their father had chosen for them, and their sons, Constantine's grandsons, had been expected to follow a similar path.

Attending university in England was flying in the face of the establishment, and, although Alex had defended his son's position, he, too, had had his doubts. But Tony was not like him; and even Constantine had had to accept that Lucia had been unstable.

And, for reasons that had more to do with the resentment he felt towards his father than for Tony's feelings, Alex had stood firm. If his son favoured his grandmother's country, why not? He himself lived and

70

worked in London these days. He would be there if Tony needed him.

His lips twisted. But he hadn't been there. In the three years since Tony left home, he had seen his son only a handful of times. It wasn't all his fault. Tony had made friends at the university, or so he'd said, and holidays had been spent skiing in Colorado, or hitch-hiking round Europe. They hadn't lost touch, exactly, but Tony hadn't seemed to want to spend time at home—at *either* of his homes, his father's or his grandfather's. And Alex had had commitments of his own. As the European vice-president of the Thiarchos corporation, he travelled quite a lot himself. And never at any time had Tony intimated that he was thinking of getting married, that he had *got* married. Or that he might be desperate enough to take his own life . . .?

He drove over the bridge that separated the town from the university, and entered the sprawling campus. A lake, dotted with swans, formed a pretty centrepiece to the various faculties, and there were numerous signs and name-plates, indicating the different departments. He avoided the lane that would have led him more directly to the administration building. He had no wish to pass the spot where his son had died. It was hard enough, coming back here. He had originally intended never to set foot on this campus again.

For the first time since he left London that morning, he allowed himself to think about Elizabeth Ryan—no, *Haley*. In all of this she was the one sane thing he had to hang on to. He knew she didn't feel that way. He knew she would rather he stayed the hell out of her life. But, dammit, she owed him an explanation, and one way or another he was determined to get it.

Not that she was the reason he had made this journey, he assured himself. Her departure from London might have caught him unawares, but he would have had to come here anyway. He still needed to talk to his daughter-in-law. Really talk to her, that was. And convince her that she owed the family something. Even if she didn't intend to pursue the association.

He saw a sign indicating the English building and, against his will, his nerves tightened. Was that where *she* worked? he wondered, fighting the urge to go and find her. Miss Elizabeth Haley, he thought disparagingly. English graduate, English lecturer, English tutor. And what else? English hustler? English harlot? English *whore*? No! Whatever else she might be, she was not promiscuous. When he'd had sex with her, she'd been a virgin. So what had she been doing, seducing him, when it was obvious she'd have no shortage of admirers here?

At first, he'd been suspicious. Even when he'd discovered that she'd covered her tracks so completely, he'd been sure there had to be more to it. He'd waited for her to contact him. Checked every message on his answerphone; examined every letter. But time, and his own lack of success in tracing her, had forced him to accept that she didn't intend to get in touch with him again. That was why seeing her at Tony's funeral had been so astounding. Why since then he hadn't been able to get her out of his mind.

But first, Linda, he reminded himself, driving past the turn-off to the English department, and continuing on to the administration block. Her determination not to take anything from the family had increased his respect for her, and, almost against his will, he felt some sympathy for her. But she was Tony's widow—his widow!— and, as such, she had some responsibilities. Not least, the need to show his grandfather some respect, by travelling to Greece to meet him...

Beth was in her office, trying to concentrate on the pile of English papers in front of her, when one of the secretaries put her head round the door.

'You've got a visitor, Beth. Is it convenient?'

Beth's mouth went dry. 'Oh?' she managed casually. 'Who is it?' Though she was sure she already knew.

'He says he's Tony Thiarchos's father,' the young woman replied, edging into the room, and pressing the door almost closed behind her. Then, in a whisper, 'My God! Have you seen him? He doesn't look old enough to have had a son Tony's age. Though I must admit he looks a bit haggard. Still, that's understandable, isn't it? In the circumstances.'

'Just show him in, Heather.' Beth was relieved to find her voice sounded almost normal. 'I—er—I was expecting him.'

'You were?'

Heather looked intrigued now, and, realising she was in danger of starting rumours she would rather not have to deal with, Beth quickly explained. 'He's come to talk about Linda,' she said, pushing back her chair and getting rather stiffly to her feet. 'Oh—and do you think you could bring us some tea?'

Heather looked rather less enthusiastic about this request, but her curiosity evidently got the better of her. 'Tea as in cups, or on a tray?' she enquired, opening the door again. Then, raising her hand defensively, 'All right. On a tray.' She glanced behind her. 'You can go in, Mr Thiarchos. Miss Haley will see you now.'

He was wearing casual clothes: a dark blue polo shirt, and close-fitting dark blue chinos. It was the first time she had seen him in casual clothes since the night of the party. At the funeral, and later, at Mrs Adams's house, he had been wearing a suit. The same suit, if she remembered correctly. Dark, and severe, and very different from what he was wearing now. It brought back a flood of memories, unwelcome memories, that she was trying to forget. Memories of him tearing off his shirt and jeans, and exposing his lean, muscled body. Memories of him coming down on the bed beside her, and of the hot, hard length of him inside her...

She bent her head for a moment, struggling to control her wayward senses. This wouldn't do, she told herself. How could she help Linda, or herself, if she allowed his appearance to upset her? He was only a man, for heaven's sake. And she had been dealing with men all her adult life. Successfully, too, until this moment—including that traumatic night in London.

Lifting her head, she forced her features into a polite mask. 'Mr Thiarchos,' she said, gesturing towards the chair at the other side of the desk. 'Won't you sit down?'

Much to her relief he did, crossing one ankle over his knee, and resting one hand on the junction. His other hand hung loosely over the arm of the chair, and, were it not for the hostile glitter of his eyes, she'd have thought he was perfectly relaxed.

But he said nothing, and, realising he was leaving it to her to choose the direction their conversation was to take, she gripped the desk and lowered herself into her seat.

'You've come to talk about Linda, of course,' she said, striving for an informal detachment, and one dark brow lifted. He was very dark, she thought unwillingly. Would her baby be as dark as he was, when it was born?

'Have I?'

His response was not what she had expected, and she swallowed. 'Well—haven't you?' she ventured. 'I understood she had left a message for you at Reception.'

Alex's eyes were disturbingly intent. 'My daughter-in-law did leave a message to the effect that you wanted to see me,' he conceded. 'You say it's to talk about Linda. I say we have other matters to discuss.'

'What—other matters?' Beth's throat felt unbearably dry. 'I doubt anything's more important than how Linda feels at the moment. She's a very mixed-up young woman, Mr Thiarchos, and——'

'Alex,' he interrupted her abruptly, and she had the feeling he hadn't listened to a word she was saying. 'The name's Alex,' he repeated, regarding her with cold dispassion. 'It's a little late for you to start calling me Mr Thiarchos, isn't it—*Liz*?'

'Beth,' she corrected him hurriedly. 'I'm called Beth. I'd rather you used that name, if you insist on the informality. But I'll call you Mr Thirachos, if you don't mind? It wouldn't be wise for us to be seen to be—to be—too familiar.'

'As in lovers?' he suggested scornfully, and her eyes sped anxiously to the door. Heather could come back with the tea at any time, and she dreaded to think of the gossip, if the secretary should overhear something like that.

'We—we were not lovers,' she declared, in a horrified undertone. 'And I'd be grateful if you wouldn't make such outrageous statements here! I've agreed to talk to you on Linda's behalf, but that's all. Now, can we stick to the real reason you've come here, and try to sort things out for her sake?'

'You condescending bitch!' Alex's expression had hardened ominously, and Beth knew the first real taste of fear. 'What if I tell you I don't give a damn about how Linda feels? My son's dead! I have to deal with that. I'm only here because of *our* relationship.'

Beth quivered. 'We—don't have a relationship,' she insisted steadily, though his harsh words had robbed her of all strength. 'Mr Thiarchos—please; I don't want this to go any further. If—if your son was still alive, we'd never have seen one another again.'

'Yes, you made damn sure of that, didn't you?' he snarled, and any hope she had had of keeping this conversation civil went out the window. She should not have let Linda persuade her to speak to him, she thought weakly. She should have remembered how angry he had been after the funeral.

'Tea up,' carolled Heather, sailing into the room without knocking, and watching her, as she put the tray on the desk, Beth tried to gauge if she had heard anything she shouldn't. But what could she have heard? she reflected bitterly, managing a tight smile of thanks. Only that Alex Thiarchos was angry, and she must think that that was understandable, in the circumstances.

'Can I get you anything else?'

Heather seemed disposed to linger now, her eyes resting on Beth's visitor with evident admiration. To his credit, Alex Thiarchos did nothing to encourage her interest, other than get politely to his feet at her entrance. A courtesy that Heather approved of, judging by the warm smile she cast in his direction. But Beth felt a surge of resentment towards both of them, and her tone was barely civil when she made a curt disclaimer.

'I'll go, then,' said Heather, her expression mirroring her disappointment as she flounced towards the door. 'If you need any more hot water, you'll have to get it yourself, Beth. I'm leaving in five minutes. I've got a dental appointment.'

Her flare of spite was almost a relief to Beth, reflecting, as it did, her curiosity about the visitor. Beth felt sure, if she had heard something untoward, she would have used it. In some ways, Heather was very transparent.

The door closed behind her with a decided bang, and in other circumstances Beth would have shared her amusement with Alex. But there was nothing amusing about the present situation, and she didn't think his decision not to resume his seat meant that the worst was over.

Trying to concentrate on the tray she had drawn towards her, Beth endeavoured not to feel threatened when Alex walked across the room to the window. The fact that the long windows were partly behind her desk was only incidental, she told herself. But her hand trembled anyway as she attempted to pour the tea.

'M-milk and sugar?' she enquired, annoyed to hear the tremor in her voice, and Alex half turned, his hands thrust into his trouser pockets.

'Neither,' he said shortly, and at her startled look, 'I don't want any tea.' Then, less aggressively, 'For God's sake, Beth, why did you do it?'

She didn't insult him by pretending not to understand what he was talking about, but it was difficult to find a convincing answer all the same. 'It was a—a spur-of-the-moment thing,' she said, which wasn't totally untrue.

'I didn't know how it would turn out, did I? It—it was just one of those things.'

'No.'

His denial was flat, and uncompromising, and to give herself time to think she pretended not to understand. 'Yes, it was,' she said quickly. 'These things—happen. I'm sure it's not the first time a—a woman's——'

'Made a pass? Seduced me?' he supplied, when it became obvious she didn't know how to go on. 'Well, believe it or not, it was the first time a woman's come on to me so—expressively. You were hot, Beth. Believe me, I remember. What doesn't make any sense is why you did it. Were you really so desperate to lose your virginity?'

'Stop it!' Beth couldn't bear for him to talk about what had happened so unemotionally, so clinically. 'All right. So I did behave badly. It must have been the drinks I'd had. I hardly ever touch alcohol——'

'No.' His denial was just as inflexible as before, and her heart hammered painfully against her ribs. 'If anyone suffered the effects of alcohol it was me, not you. And it wasn't an accident, Beth. It was planned. Down to the finest detail.'

Beth had been about to lift her cup to her lips, but now she pushed it violently away. She was trembling so much, she was sure she'd spill at least half of it over herself, and she musn't let him see how upset she was.

'Well?' he prompted at last, removing his hands from his pockets, and coming to rest them squarely on her desk. 'Don't you think I deserve an explanation? Or do you think you have the right to violate a man's body at will?'

'Vi—violate?' Beth lifted her head to look at him incredulously. That he should used that word, *her* word. 'I didn't violate you!'

'Didn't you?' His eyes were dark and unfathomable, twin pools of sable opacity. 'Well, what would you call drugging a man with strong spirits, and then taking advantage of his weakness? If I'd done that to you, Beth, what would you have called it then?'

Beth dragged her eyes away from his, and looked down at her hands, torturously clasped on the desk in front of her. 'That's different.'

'How is it different?'

'You know it is.' Her voice almost broke, and she had to steel herself to go on. 'Look—all right. I'm sorry. Maybe I shouldn't have let it happen. But it did. It's over. There's nothing I can do about it.'

'Yes, there is, dammit,' he swore angrily. 'You can tell me what the hell you did it for. Did someone bribe you? Did someone force you to do it? Is someone else behind this?'

Beth's breath escaped on a sob. 'Hardly.'

'What do you mean, hardly? Either they are or they aren't.' Alex grasped her chin with his hard fingers and forced her to look up at him. 'Answer me, dammit! It's not as crazy as you think.'

'It is crazy!' she exclaimed, pushing his hand away. 'And don't do that. Don't touch me. I don't have to tell you anything.'

'Oh, yes, you do.' Alex's mouth was a grim line. 'Unless you want me to make things very difficult for you around here, I suggest you think again.'

Beth held up her head. 'You can't threaten me.'

'Can't I?'

'No.' And then, as he still looked sceptical, she continued, 'I'm leaving at the end of this term. I shan't be returning to Sullem Cross after the summer holidays.'

Alex's eyes narrowed. 'Where are you going then?'

Beth gasped. 'Do you think I'd tell you?' And then, as the realisation that he couldn't hurt her washed over her, she added, 'My plans are not for publication. Now, shall we begin again?'

'All right.' Alex straightened. 'You want to talk about Linda, we'll talk about Linda. Go ahead.'

His sudden capitulation should have reassured her, but it didn't. It had been too quick, too easy. And there was something about his eyes, about his expression, that left her with the uneasy feeling that the worst wasn't over yet.

But, 'Won't you sit down again?' she invited, feeling far too intimidated with him looming over her. 'Perhaps you'll change your mind about the tea. It's still hot.'

Alex's expression didn't change, but he walked round the desk again, and sat down. 'No tea,' he declared, resuming his previous position. 'Don't you have any Chivas Regal hidden in your cupboard?'

Beth felt the heat invade her throat and was glad the blouse she was wearing had a high neck. But he wasn't going to disconcert her again, she thought determinedly. Even if his deliberate mockery left her feeling raw.

'About Linda,' she said, running her fingers along the sides of the papers she had been reading, and shuffling them into a neater pile, 'she says you want her to meet Tony's grandfather.'

The fleeting glance she cast in his direction caught the momentary spasm of pain that crossed his dark face at her words, but his response was as cool and unemotional as before. 'My father, yes,' he said. 'He lives on the coast, just south of Athens.'

'Yes.' Beth moistened her lips, desperately wishing this were over. When she had conceived the—some might say crazy—notion, to get pregnant, she had never envisaged a situation like this. She had never expected to see the man again, much less find herself having to justify someone else's actions to him. *As well as her own*, she conceded silently, wishing she could be as dispassionate as he was. 'Well, that's the problem. Linda doesn't feel she can go to Greece right now.'

'Doesn't she?'

His response was hardly what she had expected, but she was learning not to take what he said at face value. She had the uncomfortable feeling he was just playing with her at the moment, and for all her brave defiance she still felt apprehensive.

And, when he made no attempt to elaborate, she felt obliged to try and explain Linda's feelings. 'I think—I think she's got a lot on her mind at the moment,' she offered. 'I mean, aside from everything else, there's her exams.'

'She doesn't have to take them.'

Alex's response was flat and unemotional, but Beth didn't miss the resolution behind it. He wasn't questioning her judgement. He wasn't even denying Linda's state of mind. But he expected his will to prevail in the end.

Drawing a breath, she set the papers she had been fidgeting with aside, and as she did so her gaze settled on the cup of tea, congealing on the tray. It had obviously gone cold. There was even a little slick of grease across its surface, as if the milk Heather had given her hadn't been entirely fresh. It certainly didn't look drinkable. In fact, it looked quite disgusting. And as the perspiration beaded on her forehead she felt the familiar queasiness in her stomach.

Oh, not now, she thought sickly, pushing the tray aside, and trying to get her mind back on track. She couldn't be sick now. Not with Alex Thiarchos watching her so closely. After all, he was a father—how many times over, she had no idea. He could, conceivably, recognise the symptoms. What would she do if he guessed what was wrong with her?

'Are you all right?'

His question caught her unawares, and she gripped the edge of her desk with both hands. The carved indentations in the wood dug into her fingers, and she prayed the pain she was deliberately inflicting on herself would make the nausea go away.

'I'm—fine,' she managed, after a moment, though she doubted he believed her. 'Um—what do you mean, Linda doesn't have to take her exams? She does if she wants to get her degree.'

Alex looked as if he would have preferred to pursue his previous question, but he let her get away with it.

'She can take the exams next year, if it's so important to her,' he responded dismissively. 'But she is my son's widow, Miss Haley.' His lips twisted. 'As such, she will have no need to support herself.'

Beth felt the sickness receding, and relaxed her hands a little. 'I'm sure you know that Linda wants nothing from you——' she began, but he didn't let her finish.

'Unfortunately, she does not have a choice,' he declared harshly, his eyes no less intent. 'My mother chose to make Tony her heir. As his widow, Linda will receive the income from the trust she left to his children.'

Beth was stunned. 'Does—does Linda know this?'

Alex shrugged. 'I tried to tell her in London. She wouldn't listen. I suggest you make it clear to her. It's not going to go away.'

Beth shook her head. 'I didn't know.'

'No. I guessed not.' Alex uncrossed his legs, and came to his feet again in a lithe easy motion. 'So—I suggest we get out of here, and go some place where we can talk about it. It's obvious you're not feeling well, and I think we could both use some fresh air.'

Beth gazed up at him, aghast. 'I—I can't do that.'

'You can, if you want me to go easy on my new daughter-in-law.'

Beth caught her breath. 'But—that's blackmail!'

Alex looked down at her. 'Want to call me on it?'

Beth looked away. 'No.'

'That's what I thought.' Alex came round the desk, and put his hand beneath her elbow to assist her to her feet. 'Come on, you can show me where you really live. And I don't mean that sleazy apartment in London that you rented in an assumed name.'

CHAPTER FIVE

BETH didn't want to take Alex to her house, but she didn't really have a choice. Short of causing the kind of scene she most wanted to avoid, she was obliged to do as he had suggested. But she didn't know what he wanted with her; why he couldn't just leave well enough alone. He knew who she was now. He knew where she worked and where she lived. He knew everything about her. Everything except perhaps the most important thing, she acknowledged tensely. But dear God, that wasn't even on his agenda, so what did he want from her now?

He agreed to follow her from the university, and she was aware of the silver-grey Mercedes close behind her as she drove home. She thought of trying to give him the slip. Her pulses raced at the idea. In the maze of one-way streets around the small market town, she was sure she could get away from him. But what good would that do? she asked herself wearily. He had only to park outside her home. Sooner or later, she was bound to come back.

It was late afternoon when they arrived at Albert Terrace. The trees across the square were casting long shadows over the pavement, and already there were children playing on the grass. A couple of dogs ran, barking noisily, past the car, as she gathered her belongings, and, getting out, locked the door. Everything looked normal, she thought despairingly. Only she knew it wasn't.

Yet, as Alex parked his car behind hers, and slid out from behind the wheel, her stomach clenched in sudden anticipation. She looked down at her feet as she stepped up on to the kerb, to avoid his all too knowing eyes, but the awareness she felt in his presence just wouldn't go away. Had she really seduced this man? she wondered disbelievingly. Had she really flirted with him, and teased him, and made him want her so much that he had been prepared to risk anything to have her? Had she really gone to bed with him, and let him do to her all the things she had hitherto convinced herself she would never permit? How had she done it? How had she found the courage to achieve such a thing? And with a man like Alex Thiarchos, moreover; a man probably well-versed in the ways of women.

Only she hadn't known he *was* Alex Thiarchos at that time, she reminded herself bitterly, as she inserted her key in her front door. He had just been Alex Thorpe, a man older, but otherwise no different from the other men at the party. He had been alone, and lonely, or so she'd thought. She shook her head. Oh, Beth, she chided herself, how more wrong could you be?

'Is this one of the university houses?' Alex asked, as she took her key out of the door, and stood aside for him to step into the hall beside her, and Beth gave him an indignant look.

'No,' she denied hotly, and it was not until he acknowledged her reply with a wry grimace that she realised she should have been more discreet. So, he knew she owned a house, she consoled herself impatiently. If she hadn't told him, someone else would have.

'Mmm,' he murmured, letting her close the door behind him. 'I like it. Mid-Victorian, isn't it?'

'Do Greeks know about things like that?' Beth retorted, deciding she could afford to be a little less circumspect now that they were away from the university buildings, and Alex gave her tolerant look.

'Half-Greeks do,' he responded, without rancour. 'My mother was as English as you are.'

'How do you know I am English?' she countered, leading the way along the hall. She opened the door into the sitting-room. 'Would you wait in here, please?'

'Why do I have to wait?' He tucked his hands into the back pockets of his trousers and regarded her with cool appraising eyes. 'Where are you going?'

Beth felt the hot colour invade her neck again. 'Would you believe—the bathroom?' she enquired, with more confidence than she was feeling, and Alex shrugged.

'If you say so.' He looked into the sitting-room with a critical eye. 'This is very—formal. Do you mind if I look around?'

'Yes, I mind.' Beth gazed at him frustratedly, and then flinched back in alarm when his hand came to loop an errant strand of hair behind her ear.

'Then don't,' he advised her smoothly, and she noticed as she had before how big he was. Or perhaps it was the narrow confines of her hall. Either way, his nearness was becoming increasingly intimidating.

'You can't do this,' she protested, and his hand dropped carelessly to his side.

'I don't think you're in any position to tell me what I can or can't do,' he informed her pleasantly. 'Don't worry. I won't pry into your personal effects.'

Beth was breathing quickly, but short of attacking him with her fists there was little she could do. She supposed Pandora must have felt a little as she did, after she had opened the forbidden box. But heavens, who could have anticipated this would happen? And why, when she resented him so much, did she feel so weak every time he touched her?

And, as going to the bathroom had become such a frequent option since she'd discovered she was pregnant, Beth didn't have time to stand and debate the subject. Besides, what could he find? This was her home. Not her doctor's office.

Brushing past him, she started up the stairs, and although he turned his head to watch her she determinedly ignored him. He'd soon get tired of baiting her, if she didn't give him any satisfaction. It was her frustration that amused him; the feeling that he had her where he wanted her.

In the bathroom, she bathed her face and washed her hands. She thought of changing into more casual clothes: jeans, for instance, and an oversized T-shirt, but she dismissed the idea as being unwise. In her regular working attire of dark suit and white blouse, she felt protected. A futile presumption, perhaps, but the only one she could count on.

She did kick off her shoes, however. That was something she always did, as soon as she got home. It was only as she was going down the stairs again that she regretted the impulse. Facing Alex Thiarchos in her stockinged feet would only add to his advantage.

Still, it was too late now, and besides, as she walked along the hall and into the kitchen, she was soon more concerned with wondering where her unwelcome guest could be. A glance into both the sitting- and dining-rooms had assured her he wasn't there, and the kitchen was empty, too. He surely couldn't have left without her knowing it, could he? she wondered, aware of a curious mixture of expectation and regret. Though why she should feel any trace of dismay at his departure she couldn't imagine. The man was trouble, and she knew it. *Didn't she?*

She was trying, not very successfully, to come to terms with the complexity of her reaction when a cool draught of air fanned her face. The back door was open, she saw, and suddenly the explanation for Alex's apparent disappearance became clear. He hadn't gone. He hadn't taken pity on her, or decided he had tormented her long enough. He had just stepped outside, that was all. Into the enclosed rear garden.

She went to the door and then, remembering she wasn't wearing any shoes, she back-tracked to the window. And she saw him at once. He had found the gazebo, which had been in such a dire state of repair when Beth bought the house, and which she had had restored to its earlier beauty. He was standing in the doorway, one hand raised to support himself against the rose-covered trellis above his head, and her heart slammed into her ribs at the feeling of relief it gave her. Dear God, perhaps she shouldn't be asking herself what he wanted of her. Perhaps she should reverse that to what she wanted of him.

It had to be nothing, of course, she told herself disparagingly, disgusted at the direction her thoughts were taking. Just because she was pregnant, and because of that inclined to be more emotional than usual, she was letting her hormones run away with her reason. It was nothing to do with the fact that he looked tired, or that there was a curiously defeated expression on his face. This had been a difficult time for him. It would have been a difficult time for anybody. She mustn't start feeling sorry for him. She mustn't start getting *involved*.

But still she lingered, watching him with drawn, anxious eyes. It was only natural that she should want to comfort him, she assured herself impatiently. In heaven's name, his son was dead. In any other circumstances, she wouldn't have hesitated to offer him her sympathy.

And then he saw her in the window. She knew the moment he realised he was being observed by the way his body reacted. His air of weary introspection disappeared, and he came down the steps from the gazebo, and across the lawn, with deliberate intention. He moved easily, his long legs covering the distance with a loose athletic pace. Long, powerful legs, she noticed, almost inconsequentially, and then hurriedly reached for the kettle as he came through the door.

'Would you like some tea?'

She was concentrating on filling the kettle, and she wasn't aware of him moving behind her until his hands gripped her waist. 'I'd rather try something stronger,' he murmured huskily, as his lips brushed her cheek, and the kettle crashed into the sink as she whirled away from him.

'Don't do that!' she gasped, all thought of comforting him shattered by the simple panic his touch engendered. And then, realising her reaction had been far too extreme, she added, 'You—you startled me!

'Didn't I, though?' Alex regarded her between narrowed lids. 'And if I hadn't? Startled you, I mean. You wouldn't have objected?'

'No—I—well, yes.' Beth's tongue stumbled over the words. 'Oh, please—this is getting us nowhere. Can't we confine ourselves to finding a solution to Linda's problems? What—what happened between us isn't relevant here.'

'You think not?'

His dark eyes mocked her, and when he lifted his hand to massage the muscles at the back of his neck she started uncontrollably. For a moment, she thought he was going to touch her again, and she wasn't totally convinced she could handle him in this mood.

'I—I think you should listen to what Linda told me,' she insisted, trying not to notice that his forearm was lean and muscular, or that the colour of his hair was repeated in the fine hairs that darkened his skin. 'For instance, did you know that—that Tony had taken drugs? Or that he'd borrowed money to finance his habit?'

At last she had his undivided attention. '*What*?'

His disbelief was not feigned, and, realising she hadn't gone about this in a very tactful way, she gestured towards the hall behind her. 'Why—why don't we go and sit down and talk about it?' she suggested, licking her dry lips. 'Linda——'

'It's a lie!'

His harsh denunciation broke into her attempt to soften the blow, and this time, when his hands grasped her shoulders, there was no way she could escape from his hold. His fingers dug into her shoulders, the silky fabric of her blouse offering little protection, and his breath fanned her face, moist, and hot, and bitter.

'It—it is true,' she stammered, aware of so many things in that moment. Not least, the errant weakness she had to lean against him, to feel his strength and feed from it, instead of trembling in his grasp.

'Linda told you this?'

'Yes.'

Beth's neck was aching from the effort of holding herself aloof, and she couldn't help wondering if Linda had wanted her to talk to him for just this reason. She must have known what Tony's father's reaction would be. She must have guessed he wouldn't take this without proof.

Alex's expression was grim. 'I don't believe it,' he said again, but there was less conviction in his denial now. 'Hell—he would have told me! I'm his father, for God's sake!'

'I'm sorry.'

There was nothing else she could say, and the sympathy she had felt for him earlier flooded back at this obvious confusion. Maybe she shouldn't have told him, she thought. There was little he could do about it now. But surely he deserved to know the truth. It might even help to alleviate his pain.

'What else did she tell you?'

He was shaking her gently now, not letting her go, but reminding her, if any reminder was needed, that he was still in command. His tone was calmer, though, less aggressive, and she focused on the knot of hair, exposed by the open collar of his shirt.

'She said—she said Tony—didn't get on with his grandfather,' she admitted at last, modifying exactly what Linda had said. 'I think—I think she feels there—there might have been some—pressure on him to—to do well in his exams.'

Alex's mouth hardened. 'From whom?'

Beth bit her lip. 'I'm not sure.'

'Did she say my father had been in contact with Tony?'

'Maybe.' Beth was loath to place blame when she didn't know all the facts. 'In any case, it happened some time ago. The drug taking, I mean. According to Linda, Tony had kicked the habit before—before they got together.'

'Hmm.'

Alex appeared to be considering what she had told him, and to her relief his gaze drifted away from her taut face. But her momentary sense of reprieve was tempered when his eyes dipped lower. It was impossible to hide the shocked arousal of her body, and even though she was wearing a bra her beaded nipples were clearly visible, pressing against her blouse. Relax, she chided herself. He's not thinking about you. He's thinking about his son. But her body wouldn't obey her commands, and she guessed he was aware of it.

'Tell me about her,' he said suddenly, and his words were in such counterpoint to her fears that she could only stare at him.

'About who?'

'Linda, of course,' he said patiently, watching his thumbs trace a sensuous path against her shoulder. 'What do you think of her? What kind of a person is she?'

Beth caught her breath. 'You've met her.'

'I've met many of Tony's friends.' Alex grimaced. 'Believe it or not, my son was not a stranger to me. We—had our differences, I'll admit. But what father can say he hasn't had differences with his son? I thought he was happy. I thought he was content with his life here in England. You can have no conception of how I felt when I heard that Tony was dead.'

Beth thought perhaps she could. She remembered how she had felt when her sister died, but that was many years ago, and not something she wanted to remember. She had to stop finding associations between his life and hers. As soon as this was over, she would never see him again.

'And that's why I need to know more about the woman who was my son's wife,' Alex continued evenly. 'She won't let me near her. I don't even know where they were married, or if there might be repercussions from the liaison I'm not even aware of.'

'Repercussions?'

'A child,' said Alex harshly, his disturbing eyes returning to her parted lips. 'My daughter-in-law may be pregnant. And, selfish as it might seem, I should not want my grandchild being brought up without my knowledge!'

Beth's breath escaped on a sigh. 'She's not,' she said swiftly.

Alex's brows compressed. 'You asked her?'

'Yes.' Beth swallowed. 'I realise it's none of my business, but I wondered if—if that was why——'

'She didn't want to see me?'

Beth hesitated. 'Well—yes.'

A spasm of pain crossed his face then and, with a muttered exclamation, he let go of her and turned away. 'So,' he said bitterly, 'it's finished. I have no son and no prospective grandson.' He cast a mocking glance over his shoulder. 'You see a man without heirs, Miss Haley. An unforgivable sin in my father's eyes.'

Beth tried to regulate her breathing. 'You could—marry again.'

His lips twisted. 'I think not.'

'Why not?'

He shrugged. 'Because I do not appear to be very good at sustaining relationships,' he replied bleakly. 'My wife left me for another man; my son is dead—who knows how, or why?—my daughter-in-law won't even speak to me, and you...' he paused '...you did your best to ensure I'd never find you again.'

Beth shook her head. 'Why should you want to find me?' she protested, and he swung about to face her.

'Why not?' he demanded, flinging her own words back at her. 'Surely you knew how I would feel when I discovered the apartment was empty. My God, are you completely without conscience? Do you know what that did to my ego?'

Beth tilted her head. 'That's what all this is about? Your ego?'

His eyes darkened. 'You know it's not.'

Beth faltered. His words, and the disturbing intensity of his gaze, were causing all manner of warning bells to go off inside her head. Keep calm, she told herself, he's only playing with you. But the memories she had kept at bay were sweeping into her mind. Memories of heat, and warmth, and passion; of shadowy bodies locked and merging, of feverish words, and slick skin, and the moist, pulsing power of his possession...

She tried to escape it. She tried to speak coolly, using a slightly sardonic tone to disguise her inner torment. 'I—I can't believe you found the experience so—so unforgettable,' she quipped, hoping to incite his defiance. But Alex's response was to grasp her upper arm, and this time when he held her there was fire in his touch.

'Don't make fun of me, Beth,' he warned, and for the first time since that night at the flat she feared the consequences of her actions. 'I may not have been the dream lover of your fantasies,' he continued, 'but it was good between us. More than good, damn you, for all your crazy games!'

'*My* games!'

Beth could hardly get the words out, and he used her shocked reaction to turn her into his arms. 'Well, what would you call them?' he demanded huskily, grasping her wrists and taking them behind her back. He thrust his face close to hers. 'What else would drive an apparently sober-minded academic to act like a cheap tart?'

Beth gasped. 'It wasn't like that!' she exclaimed, though she could quite see why he would think it was. But at that moment she was more concerned with extricating herself from her present predicament than finding excuses for his accusations. 'Don't do this,' she begged, as his hot breath fanned her ear. 'Alex, isn't this rather childish? Let me go, please!'

'That's not what you said that night,' he taunted, taking the lobe of her ear between his teeth. He bit down, hard, causing a little whimper of protestation to pass her lips. 'As I remember, you were desperate for my body. Desperate for me to touch you...' He matched his actions to his words, using his hold on her wrists to urge her even closer. 'Desperate for me to kiss you...' His lips slid along the resisting line of her jaw, reaching their

objective when she couldn't turn her head any further.
'Desperate for me to—what shall we call it?—*love* you?'
His mouth brushed her lips. 'Oh, yes, you were desperate for that all right. But let's call it by it's proper
name, shall we?'

'You're disgusting!' she cried, the word he whispered
in her ear causing her to fight against his grasp.
Desperate, too, to prevent him from discovering exactly
how vulnerable she was. It was hard enough to parry his
insults, when she could use the authority of her position
at the university as a defence. It would be impossible if
she betrayed herself here.

But, hampered as she was by his possession of her
wrists and the proximity of his body, there was little she
could do when his mouth slanted across hers. And, for
a dizzying moment, she didn't want to deny him. His
lips were hard, but not brutal, his tongue stroking along
her teeth, causing her lips to part. Her jaw sagged, and
weakness had her leaning into him, arching against him,
seeking to prolong the moist melding of their mouths.
For a brief spell, her senses spun out of her control, and
he made a hoarse sound that was half-elation, half-
defeat.

It was that, as much as anything, that brought a
chilling awareness of what she was doing. No, not what
she was doing, what she was allowing to happen, she
corrected herself fiercely. She couldn't blame herself for
his behaviour. He was controlling the situation, not her.

'Let me go!'

With a supreme effort she fought free of him but the
ease with which she escaped his grasp surprised her. One
moment, he had been possessing her wrists, urging her
against his taut body, making her aware of his own
arousal, and the next she was standing, swaying, almost
lost without his support.

Alex, meanwhile, was watching her with a vaguely
contemptuous expression. It was obvious he knew exactly
how she was feeling. She hadn't fooled him with her
futile protestations. He had felt her weakness, but for
some reason best known to himself he had not chosen

to take advantage of it. She had the unpleasant suspicion she was going to find out why.

'I—think you said something about tea,' he remarked suddenly, and Beth felt her charged emotions spin into confusion. What now? she wondered unsteadily. How could he think about tea, when only moments before...?

But that kind of thinking would get her nowhere. Maybe the worst was over, she thought, discovering a button on her blouse was undone, and hurriedly restoring it to its proper place as she moved towards the sink. She had done what she had promised to do: she had told him about Tony, and endeavoured to explain Linda's reasons for avoiding a confrontation. Whether or not he understood her position, whether he even *believed* her, was not her problem. What she had to do now was behave as normally as possible; and get him out of her house, before she made some irreparable mistake...

The kettle was lying on its side in the sink where she had dropped it, and she rescued it with trembling fingers, and filled it from the tap. Then, realising that it was foolish actually to *fill* the kettle, when every minute it took to boil would only prolong her nervousness, she half emptied it again, before attaching it to the plug.

'I wouldn't have thought Greeks drank tea,' she ventured, in an effort to restore some normality to the situation, and then started, when he pulled out a chair from the small pine table, where she ate most of her meals, and, straddling it, sat down.

'Half-Greeks do,' he responded, reminding her once again that his ancestry was mixed. 'Besides,' he continued, 'you know almost nothing about my likes and dislikes. Ironic, isn't it? We've slept together, but we haven't exchanged much small talk.'

Beth fumbled the tea caddy out of the cupboard, only saving it from spilling into the sink, too, with an effort. 'Perhaps that's because you can't talk about anything else but what happened that night in London,' she retorted unguardedly. Then, with some impatience at her own recklessness, she added, 'It's been a lovely day, hasn't it? British summers seem to be getting better and better.'

'Do they?' His response was coolly mocking. 'Well, Greek summers are good, too. And, dare I say it, more reliable? Much like Greeks themselves. More honest, anyway.'

Beth turned on him then. 'There you go again,' she exclaimed, the tautness of her nerves giving her a spurious courage. 'I've apologised for what I did. What more do you want me to say? I'm sorry if I hurt your pride. I didn't know it would be you.'

Alex's eyes narrowed, fixing her with a dark compelling gaze. 'You didn't know *what* would be me?' he echoed, latching on to the one inconsistency in her words, and Beth felt the hot colour flood her cheeks.

'I mean—I didn't know who you were,' she mumbled, bending over the cups she was setting on a tray, and for a moment the only sound was the water heating in the kettle.

'All right.' When she had convinced herself he must have guessed her objective, Alex spoke again. 'All right,' he said again, 'you didn't know who I was. Leaving aside the obvious comment that you were taking an appalling risk, I'm willing to make a bargain with you.'

'A bargain?' Beth looked up, but her throat was dry.

'Yes, a bargain,' said Alex smoothly, his long fingers tracing the grain of the chair. 'You persuade Linda to accompany me to Athens, and when the trip is over I won't bother you any more.'

Beth blinked. 'But she won't go! I've told you——'

'She will, if you tell her you'll go with her,' Alex interrupted her evenly, pressing down on the back of the chair, and getting to his feet. 'You can forget the tea. I've decided I'm not thirsty after all. I'll leave you to think about it. Don't come to any hasty decisions. I can be a real nuisance, believe me!'

CHAPTER SIX

EAST of Athens, beyond the sprawling suburbs of the
rapidly expanding city, the foothills of Mount Hymettus
were dotted with Byzantine shrines. Beth knew they were
Byzantine shrines, because she had read the guide book
she had bought with reluctant avidity, devouring its pages
nightly, in an effort to dull her mind. She knew that
there was a monastery at Kaisariani, and a spring shaded
by a huge plane tree. It was said that the spring had
certain powers of fertility, and even today superstitious
women came to drink its waters.

She could have bored Linda silly with all the useless
information she had absorbed about Greece. Information
about fishing and industry; about cultivating vines, and
growing olives, and catering to its ever-growing tourist
population. She had done her best to stifle any natural
curiosity she had had, and filled her head with the prosaic
facts of Greece's economy. It was only now, as they drove
up a bare winding slope towards another white-walled
monastery, that she had to acknowledge she had absorbed other things as well. Not least the awareness that
the scent drifting through the open window was from
the thyme that grew in such profusion on the hillside,
and that the flowering shrubs were interspersed with pink
and mauve anemones in the springtime. She could almost
see the delicate petals, spreading themselves so proudly,
before the blazing heat of a summer sun burned their
sweetness away. But even the browned earth had its
magic, and the vista that spread before them, when they
reached a bare plateau, was impossible to ignore.

The Aegean was spread out ahead of them, blue and
almost brittle in the clear afternoon light. The brilliance
of the light here was legendary, imbuing everything with

its radiance. Beth had the feeling she could see into infinity, as if that was the actual curvature of civilisation on the far horizon.

But then, she had had similar feelings of awe when their flight from London had circled over Athens, and she had had her first glimpse of the Acropolis. From the air, the ancient temple of Athena looked wonderfully impressive—more impressive than it did on the ground, Justine had informed her spitefully, in one of her rare bursts of confidence.

But then, Justine did not approve of Beth's trip to Greece. She considered the whole idea highly unsuitable. 'I think you're mad,' she had declared, when she discovered what Beth had reluctantly agreed to do. 'You hardly know this girl, or her in-laws, and you're planning on wasting part of your holiday in humouring her. Lord, she doesn't know when she's well off. The Thiarchoses could have washed their hands of her. Instead of which they're bending over backwards to be courteous.'

Beth could have agreed. Indeed, she had tried to change Linda's mind, not least because of her own feelings. She didn't want to go to Greece. She didn't want to spend any more time with Alex Thiarchos, or get to know him better. She already knew him far better than was good for her.

But Linda had been adamant. Not even the news about Tony's grandmother's legacy had persuaded her to do what they asked. Increasingly, Beth had had the feeling that without her participation the younger woman would have refused to allow any connection between herself and the Thiarchos family, which begged the question of why she, Beth, had permitted herself to become involved.

Of course, she had reasons to justify what she was doing. Aside from any threats Alex might have made, Constantine Thiarchos was an old man, and, whatever his sins, he must have loved his grandson very much. Surely Linda owed it to him at least to acknowledge his existence. Even if she was feeling bitter now, once the shock of Tony's death had ceased to be so painful she might regret refusing this chance to get to know her husband's family.

Or so Beth had argued, consoling herself with the belief that what she was doing was right, if not entirely sensible. It really had nothing to do with her own unwilling involvement with Alex Thiarchos; nothing to do with any latent sympathy she might feel for him, or the guilt she was suffering by keeping the knowledge of her own condition to herself. She was accompanying Linda as an impartial bystander, that was all—though only time would tell how impartial she could be.

And, of course, Linda had eventually acquiesced, accepting Beth's offer to accompany her without question. It was as if the fact that she had been there, when Tony was buried, had created a bond between them. A bond Beth told herself she was eager to break, as soon as this journey was over.

But for now, she was compelled to go through with it, warding off Linda's words of gratitude with a rueful heart. It was hard to accept her thanks for coming with her, when there was so much more involved. Hard to view what she was doing rationally, when emotion was tying her hands.

She pressed an unwary hand to the distinct swell that marked her midriff, and knew a moment's panic. Slowly, but surely, her pregnancy was beginning to show, and she realised she had been a little reckless in allowing Linda to stay and take her exams. But the girl had been so desperate not to have to return to college the following year, and Beth had had to agree that she needed to graduate, if she wanted to support herself.

To begin with, Beth had tried to tell her that she probably need never worry about supporting herself again, but Linda had been adamant. She didn't want the Thiarchoses to support her; she wanted to be independent. And how could Beth ignore that, when she had had much the same feelings when she left home?

Alex had not been pleased, of course. He hadn't returned to Sullem Cross, but Beth had received two rather
hostile phone calls. If this was some ploy she was using,
he had warned, if she thought by delaying their departure he might change his mind, she was wrong. She
had precisely three weeks to deliver Linda to Athens.
Without that affirmation, he could not answer for his
actions.

Which meant, Beth knew, that news of her unseemly
behaviour in London could reach the ears of offi-
cialdom, and, while she might try to convince herself
that she didn't care, that she was taking a sabbatical,
and his accusations couldn't hurt her, she knew it wasn't
true. They could hurt her; they could hurt her chances
of being employed again. And, with a child to support,
she couldn't afford to take the chance.

Of course, there were times, particularly in the early
morning, when she felt sure he wouldn't do anything to
hurt her, but those times were few and far between.
Besides, if she was completely honest, she would have
to admit that, Alex's threats apart, she was curious to
see where her baby's father had been born and brought
up. Her child was going to know so little about its father.
She owed it to herself to learn something of his
background.

Any anger she had felt at his high-handed manipu-
lation of her immediate future had soon dissipated. She
was doing something she believed in—at least so far as
Linda was concerned. And, after she got back to
England, she need never see Alex again. It seemed a
reasonable bargain. At any rate, it was the best she was
going to get.

But that didn't mean she had to enjoy it, she told
herself, as the chauffeur-driven limousine that had col-
lected them from the international airport in Athens
began its rugged descent towards the coast. Nevertheless,
she had to force herself to sit back in her seat as they
skirted pine-clad promontories and vineyards, with
grapes ripening in the sun. It was an effort not to re-

spond to the sight of white beaches and rocky coves, and villas gleaming white, in gardens bright with geraniums and other flowering plants. And everywhere there was the light, and the air, and an atmosphere filled with the glories of the past. Almost every hilltop had its temple or its shrine, and Beth could feel the magic of the place seeping into her bones.

'It's so hot!' Linda said beside her, fanning herself with a languid hand, and Beth dragged her eyes away from the window to give her companion a sympathetic smile.

'It is,' she agreed, though in all honesty she was revelling in the unaccustomed warmth of the July day. 'Shall I ask the driver to turn up the air-conditioning?'

'Can you?'

Linda gave her a wry look, and Beth made an apologetic gesture. 'Probably not,' she admitted, realising her smattering of schoolgirl Greek wouldn't get her very far. 'Well, it can't be much further. Al—that is, Mr Thiarchos said Vouliari was only about thirty miles from Athens. Near enough for his father to commute to his office, apparently. We'll soon be there.'

'And you think that makes me feel better?' Linda countered drily. 'Beth, I don't want to get there. I just want to go home.'

'Oh, Linda!' Beth stared at the girl with worried eyes. 'It won't be so bad. Honestly. Tony's grandfather just wants to meet you. That's natural, isn't it? In the circumstances?'

'To salve his conscience, you mean?'

'No.' Beth sighed. 'Linda, whatever Constantine Thiarchos did while Tony was alive, he's paid for it, hasn't he? No one—no one could have anticipated that Tony might—might——'

'Kill himself?' Linda spoke almost dispassionately. 'No. No one could have anticipated that.'

Beth shook her head. 'That wasn't what I meant, and you know it. No one knows how Tony died. So far as the coroner was concerned, it was an accident.'

'Was it?' Linda was sceptical. 'How can I be sure of that?'

'Look,' Beth attempted to reason with her, 'you've got to put the past behind you.'

'Why?'

'Why?' Beth stared at her. 'Because—because you have. You can't let it control the rest of your life.'

But even as she said these words Beth wondered how qualified she was to use them. She had let the past control her life. She had let her mother's betrayal and her father's bitterness turn her into an emotional cripple.

'We'll see,' Linda muttered now, staring blankly through the car window, and with that Beth had to be content.

A few minutes later, they turned off the wide coast road and followed a myrtle-strewn track fringed with evergreens. It wound down towards the beach, and then veered upwards again to a small promontory. A vine-hung gateway gave access to a shingled drive, which in turn circled a tumble of hydrangeas to reach a wide forecourt.

And then they saw the house. It was a sprawling single-storeyed dwelling, with wrap-around wings, which seemed to enclose a courtyard at the rear. Like the other villas they had seen it was painted white, with a tiled roof of dark red tiles, but there the resemblance ended. Its impressive size, and the ornate ironwork at its windows, signified that this was more than just another house. And when two men emerged from the back of the house to check on their arrival Beth had a little indication of what being a Thiarchos might mean.

'Oh, *God*!'

She had been so intent on her own feelings, she had briefly forgotten Linda's, but now Beth looked at the girl's horrified face with determinedly cheerful eyes. 'Well, we're here,' she remarked, rather obviously. 'Isn't it a beautiful spot?'

And it was. Sliding out of the car, which the chauffeur had opened for her, Beth thought she had seldom, if ever, seen a more beautiful one. They were on a narrow plateau, with the blue waters of the Aegean seemingly visible an all sides. A bay curved away to their right, and in the distance she could see the roofs and gardens of a small fishing village. Vouliari, she guessed, remembering that Alex had mentioned the nearness of the village. But closer at hand there was a shelving hillside, with lawns and gardens, and a sun-kissed cove below, where the water creamed and surged along the shoreline.

'Beautiful,' Linda echoed unenthusiastically, climbing out of the car behind her. 'But so hot!' She shaded her eyes and watched a pair of seabirds, swooping and crying overhead. 'Do you think the Thiarchoses own the village too?'

Beth glanced round, half apprehensively, but happily no one appeared to have overheard them. 'Don't be cynical,' she said, pushing her hand through the girl's arm, and trying to jolly some positive response from her. 'Just think of this as a holiday. It'll be over soon enough.'

'Will it?' Linda didn't sound as if she believed her, but she permitted herself a brief glance at the house. 'It is—nice,' she admitted unwillingly. 'Do you think Tony's father will be here to introduce me?'

Beth succeeded in suppressing her own exclamation at this enquiry, and managed a small smile. 'Oh—I shouldn't think so,' she said, realising this was something she hadn't given too much consideration to. She had been so intent on persuading Linda not to back out of their agreement, she hadn't thought of what she would do if Alex didn't keep to his. But he wouldn't be here, she told herself. He had admitted he lived and worked in London.

'*Kiria*!'

The unfamiliar form of address had both women turning to look at the person who had used it. An elderly Greek woman, dressed almost entirely in black, was standing on the forecourt, evidently waiting to escort them into the house.

'Oh——' When Linda said nothing, only looked at the woman with anxious eyes, Beth stepped forward. 'Um—*milate anglika*?'

'*Ne, kiria*, a little,' the Greek woman nodded, and Linda turned to Beth in obvious panic.

'She doesn't speak English?'

'She does. A little, anyway.'

'But she said—nay!'

'She said *ne*,' Beth amended. 'It means yes. *Ohi* means no. Didn't Tony tell you that?'

Linda shrugged. 'He may have done,' she mumbled, a little wildly. 'Oh, lord, Beth, what am I doing here? I'll never make myself understood.'

'My father speaks excellent English,' a low, attractive male voice inserted, and Beth, who would have known that voice anywhere, swung round in alarm. Just as she had suspected, Alex Thiarchos had emerged from the villa behind them, and was now standing watching them, arms crossed over his midriff, his dark face alight with satisfaction.

'Oh, Mr Thiarchos!' Abandoning Beth, Linda crossed the stretch of gravel between her and her father-in-law, and gazed at him as if he were a life-saver. The antipathy she had exhibited towards him in England seemed totally absent as she let him take her hand before kissing her on both cheeks. 'Thank goodness you're here,' she added. 'I—is Tony's grandfather waiting for us?'

'Regrettably, my father has had to return to Athens,' Alex told her smoothly, his eyes flicking to Beth's flushed face, over the younger girl's head. 'He'll be back this evening, and until then I'll do my best to entertain you.' He paused. 'Good afternoon, Miss Haley. I trust you had a pleasant journey?'

Considering they had travelled in the first-class compartment of the plane, and a chauffeur-driven limousine had been waiting to bring them to their destination, Beth didn't see how they could have had a pleasanter one. Which did not apply to reaching their destination, she thought tensely. Dear God, how long was Alex Thiarchos staying here?

But, unable to voice her feelings in Linda's presence, Beth strove for a detached courtesy. 'It was very pleasant, thank you, Mr Thiarchos. Er—we were just admiring the view. Is—is that Vouliari over there?'

Leaving his daughter-in-law to point out which suit-cases were hers, Alex strolled across to where Beth was standing. 'Vouliari,' he agreed, in a normal tone, 'and that's Cape Iannis, in the background.' Then, barely audibly, 'You're looking well. You've got colour in your cheeks. Dare I say that my country seems to agree with you?'

'I'm hot, that's all,' said Beth, rather shortly, and then, realising Linda might hear her and misinterpret her re-action, she added in an undertone, 'What are you doing here? This wasn't part of our bargain!'

'Wasn't it?' Alex's eyes were narrowed and intent, and the fingers that closed so inexorably around her arm were infuriatingly familiar. 'I don't remember saying I wouldn't be here,' he informed her huskily, and when his eyes moved to her mouth Beth sucked in an anxious breath. 'Did you really think I'd let you get away from me without sleeping with you again? Beth, I want you. Surely you didn't really think I couldn't handle Linda on my own?'

The sun sank in a blaze of apricot and gold. And, almost before the crimson orb had disappeared behind the mountains, stars were winking in a sky as soft as velvet. It was all incredibly beautiful, but Beth, watching the display from her bedroom window, was in no mood to be impressed.

Instead, she felt incredibly angry, and incredibly stupid. She had felt that way since Alex's mocking greeting, and she had spent the time it took to take a shower and dry her hair trying to find some way to get out of her predicament.

But, for the moment, there seemed no easy solution. And, no matter what Alex had said, she doubted he would have found Linda such an easy target. The girl was still protesting her unwillingness to be here, despite Alex's presence, and, should Beth make some excuse to leave, she suspected Linda would go with her.

Which should have been a relief, but wasn't. After all, she hadn't persuaded Linda to come here for Alex's benefit. His appearance was purely incidental. No, they were here because Tony's grandfather wanted to meet Linda. That hadn't changed, and wouldn't, until the old man returned.

Beth sighed. All the same, it wasn't very comfortable for her, knowing that Alex saw this as an opportunity to deal with her on his own terms. It might be his father's house, but it was his home, too. And, so long as she remained here, she was at his mercy.

At his mercy?

She shook her head impatiently. That was definitely over-dramatising the situation. She wasn't at his mercy. She wasn't at any man's mercy, and never would be. If, when she had planned to have a baby, she hadn't considered all the pitfalls, that was her fault. But it wasn't an irredeemable mistake.

And she defied anyone to have anticipated the chain of events that had brought her to this present impasse. Even in her wildest dreams, she could never have foreseen that her innocent interception of Tony Thiarchos's conversation could have had such an effect on her life. She had thought getting pregnant would the hard part. How wrong she had been!

And now Alex Thiarchos was doing his best to sabotage all she had achieved. Totally without conscience, he was planning to take advantage of her weakness, and there was nothing she could do about it.

Except tell him the truth, a small voice taunted, but that was one alternative she couldn't consider. If he found out she was carrying his baby, there would be no place she could hide. And, even if her own conscience balked at the thought, she had to keep her secret.

A knock at her door alerted her to the fact that she was still not dressed. The silky black teddy she was wearing was hardly decent, and she had no way of knowing who was waiting beyond the panels.

Snatching up the robe she had worn immediately after her shower, she hurriedly thrust her arms into the sleeves. Then, wrapping it closely about her, she tied the cord, before calling, 'Who is it?'

'Me,' came Linda's flat tone. 'Can I come in?'

Beth glanced down at herself. In a towelling bathrobe, with bare feet, and no make-up, she hardly looked like the conventional image of a university tutor. But then, these were not conventional circumstances. In any case, Linda had taken her exams, and to all intents and purposes she had ceased to be her student. When the results were published in a week or two's time, she expected to be a graduate herself.

'Yes, come in,' Beth called now, albeit somewhat unwillingly. She hadn't spoken to Linda alone since their arrival a couple of hours ago, and she suspected the girl would want to know what Alex had been saying to her so confidentially.

Linda was dressed for the evening, her wide-legged cotton trousers and tie-waisted blouse revealing her uncertainty as to the correct attire for dining at the Villa Vouliari. Her eyes widened when she saw Beth was still wearing her bathrobe, and, closing the door, she regarded her apprehensively.

'You are joining—them—for dinner, aren't you?' she exclaimed, rather anxiously. 'You don't expect me to go on my own.'

'Oh—no. No.' Beth shook her head reassuringly, wishing she had someone to reassure her. 'I've just got to put a dress on, that's all.' She managed a smile. 'And some shoes, of course.'

'Mmm.' Linda nodded, her relief palpable. Then, 'You look—different.'

'Different?' Beth kept her tone even with an effort.

'Yes.' Linda regarded her half enviously. 'Younger. More feminine, somehow.' She made a rueful grimace. 'I guess I'm used to seeing you in formal suits and blouses. Sort of like a corporate image, if you know what I mean. Even at the—even at the funeral, you didn't seem as—as approachable as you do now.'

'Oh.' Beth relaxed a little. 'You worried me there for minute.'

'Why?' Linda made a face. 'I don't think anything I could say would upset you. You're quite at home here.'

'I wouldn't say that.'

'I would.' Linda sauntered to the wide bed, and seated herself on the edge of the satin coverlet. 'This place doesn't intimidate you the way it does me. I could tell that. I mean—the way you spoke to Tony's dad, for instance. What did he say to you, anyway? You looked ever so annoyed when you came into the house.'

'Um——' Beth looped a silvery strand of hair behind her ear, and struggled to think of an answer. 'I can't remember now. I—don't think I was annoyed.' *Liar!* 'He—he was just pointing out the view, that's all.'

'Was he?' Linda didn't sound totally convinced. 'So what's he like? Really like, I mean. You've talked to him more than I have. Does he blame me for what happened? Is he angry because Tony and I got married?'

'I—think you'll have to ask him yourself, Linda.' Beth turned away, ostensibly to lift a small jar of eyeshadow from her make-up case. Unscrewing the top, she concentrated on the dusty brown substance it contained. 'He—he seems very approachable. It's up to you to convince him that you and Tony were happy.'

Linda snorted at this, a bitter, scornful sound, and Beth looked up. 'Well,' the younger girl said, scuffing her canvas-booted toe against the cream rug that lay on the shining blocks beside the bed, 'do you really think he's likely to believe me? Why didn't Tony tell his father and his grandfather about us? That's what I'd like to know. If he really loved me, if he really wanted our marriage to last, why did I never meet any of the members of his family?'

Beth frowned. 'But I thought you said——'

'That Tony was afraid of his grandfather? He was. And I know he said he hadn't told anyone about us because his family would force him to go back to Greece. But what if it wasn't true? What if Tony was lying?' She sniffed. 'Oh, Beth, I don't know what to believe any more. I just wish I hadn't had to come.'

Beth took a breath. 'Look,' she said gently, 'I shouldn't worry about it, if I were you.' *And wasn't she a fine one to make a statement like that*? 'We've had a long journey, and you're tired. It's natural that you should have some doubts. Why don't you just play the whole thing by ear? At least until you've had a chance to judge these people for yourself.'

'I suppose you're right.' Linda lifted the hem of the dress Beth had laid on the bed earlier. 'Is this what you're wearing?' She admired its scooped neckline, elbow-length sleeves, and short flaring hemline. 'Black silk. How gorgeous! I wish I'd brought something like that.'

'It's polyester, actually,' said Beth, and, realising she was not going to persuade Linda to leave without her, she took a pair of wispy black stockings out of her case, and began to draw them over her legs. It was less easy to discard the towelling bathrobe, and expose her scantily clothed figure to Linda's appraising eyes. Even without the consciousness of her thickening waistline, she was not used to dressing or undressing in front of anyone, and she saw the girl's eyes widen when she saw the teddy. Well, what did students think their tutors wore in terms of underwear? she asked herself impatiently, glad when the silky fabric of the dress slithered over her hips. Cotton bras and pants probably, she reflected, remembering her own youth with a pang. It wasn't that long since she had thought that anyone approaching thirty was well over the hill.

She was relieved to see that the weight she had lost while she was suffering from morning sickness more than

compensated for what she had gained. It hadn't occurred to her to try on the dress before putting it in her
suitcase, and she wondered what she would have said if
the midriff had been uncomfortably tight.

But such thoughts were pointless, and after using some
of the dusty brown eyeshadow and a tawny pink lipgloss
she pronounced herself ready. She ran a final brush
through her hair, which hung straight and smooth to her
shoulders, and then turned to Linda with what she hoped
was a confident smile. 'Shall we go?'

Linda stood up somewhat reluctantly. 'Do I look all
right?'

'Of course.' Beth viewed the younger girl's appearance with genuine approval. 'You look very nice,
and very pretty.'

'Do you think so?'

Linda was pathetically anxious, and Beth paused to
give her a swift hug. 'Of course,' she said, gently urging her towards the door. 'Stop worrying. They can't
hurt you.'

CHAPTER SEVEN

'So, SHE'S here!' Constantine Thiarchos regarded his younger son across the leather-topped slab of mahogany he called his desk, and ran a bony finger around the rim of his glass. 'Have you spoken to her?'

'Briefly.'

Alex was non-committal, watching his father's neutrality of expression with guarded eyes. He knew better than to think he could read anything from those swarthily cast features. Constantine was a past master at disguising his real thoughts.

'And?'

The old man expected Alex to tell him everything, while he was being less than forthright. Exactly what did he know about Tony's death that he wasn't saying?

'And nothing,' Alex answered now, unwillingly remembering that his reaction to Beth's arrival had superseded everything else. 'We hardly had a conversation. They were tired after the journey, and they were shown straight to their rooms and offered refreshments. That's about it.'

'They?' His father frowned. 'Oh, yes. This woman she's brought with her. I'd forgotten about that. What is her name? Miss Harvey?'

'Haley,' said Alex smoothly, knowing full well that his father never forgot anything, least of all the name of a woman who in his opinion had accompanied Linda for less than selfless motives. 'Her name's Elizabeth Haley. Beth, to her friends.'

Constantine's lips twisted. 'And my grandson's wife regards her as a friend? I understood she was her professor, or some such.'

'She is—*was*.'

'And now she is a friend. Most convenient, don't you think? Particularly when it affords her an expenses-paid trip to Greece, eh?'

'She's not like that.' Alex was brusque.

'How do you know?'

'I—just know.' Alex was annoyed to hear the irritation in his voice. If he wasn't careful, his father would begin to suspect he had something to hide. 'I invited her myself. Linda might not have come otherwise.'

Constantine snorted. 'If you believe that, you'll believe anything. Didn't you tell her about the legacy?'

Alex's eyes were hard. 'Of course I told her.'

'And?'

'She doesn't want to know.'

Constantine sneered. 'I don't believe it.'

'That's your prerogative.'

His father frowned, evidently not as convinced as he had pretended. 'All right,' he said. 'Suppose what you say is true. What does she want? What are her ambitions?'

Alex shrugged. 'To get her degree.'

'And after?'

'A job.' Alex swallowed the remains of the cloudy substance in his own glass, and went to pour himself another ouzo and water. 'What does it matter? She says she wants to remain independent.'

'Hmm.' The old man watched his son with narrowed eyes. 'But everyone has a price, Alexander. You should know that. Better than most.'

Alex's nostrils flared, but he didn't rise to the bait. Not this time. His father's reference to Alex's own marriage, and the ease with which he had extricated him from it, when Lucia's infidelities had begun to threaten the family's honour, no longer stung him as it had once done. Besides, he had never loved Lucia. He had never loved any woman, except his mother. And perhaps Lucia had known that, and that was why she had sought love in other relationships, he reflected, feeling unexpectedly benevolent towards his ex-wife. She seemed happy enough now with the polo player who had replaced him, and he didn't begrudge her her escape from his father's domination. Hadn't he spent all his adult life doing the same?

'So, why did you ask to meet her?' he asked now, contemplating the liquid in his glass. 'If you have such a low opinion of her morals.' His dark brows arched. 'What are you afraid of?'

His father scowled. 'Guard your tongue,' he snapped. And then, as if afraid he had been indiscreet, he added, 'Have you forgotten your grandmother had shares in the corporation? Do you think I want them to fall into the wrong hands?'

Alex shrugged. 'Your lawyers could have handled it.'

His father shifted in his chair. 'I chose to handle it myself. Besides, she was Tony's wife. I have—responsibilities.'

'Agreed.' Alex was bitter. 'I just wonder how you live with them.'

'And what is that supposed to mean?' Constantine's face was taut with resentment.

'You tell me.' Alex set his drink down on a nearby cabinet, as if the smell had suddenly repulsed him. 'Did you know about Tony's drug habit? Was that why you threatened to disown him?'

'Why I——' Constantine's jaw sagged for a moment, and then he gathered himself again. 'Alex, I've told you. I knew nothing about——'

'I know what you said,' Alex interrupted him harshly. 'But since I first asked you about that situation I've made some enquiries of my own. And you know what?' His lips twisted. 'I don't believe Tony could have done anything without one of your *mangas* finding out about it!'

'Alex——'

'And what about those letters you sent him, hmm? I know there were letters, so don't deny it.'

'Why should I?' Constantine had recovered his composure. 'Why shouldn't I write to my own grandson? There's no law against that, is there?'

Alex frowned. 'You were in England only a couple of days before Tony died.'

'And you know why.' Constantine expelled a heavy breath. 'I spent two days in London, at the European ecology conference, before flying to Madrid to see your aunt Sophie. Alex, please. Haven't we had enough grief in this family? What good is turning on one another?'

Alex turned away. 'If I thought that you had anything to do with Tony's death——'

'I didn't.' Constantine got abruptly to his feet. 'Come. It is time we made ourselves available to our guests.'

To Beth's surprise—and relief—there was no one waiting for them in the salon, to which a uniformed maid directed them. At least it would give them time to familiarise themselves with their surroundings, she thought, giving Linda's arm a squeeze. Time, too, to take up a position from which they could confront the enemy.

A foolish notion perhaps, she conceded, but one with which she was sure Linda would agree. The younger woman had been visibly shaking, as they walked along the wide corridor that led from the south wing of the house where they had been accommodated to the expansive reception hall they had seen on their arrival. This was obviously a strain for her—for both of them, Beth acknowledged drily. She just hoped she could stifle her own fears, and give Linda the support she deserved.

But then, she reflected, anyone would be intimidated by this place. Her rooms alone had a floorspace equal to the entire ground floor of her house in England. And she guessed, from what she had said as they trod the marble tiles of the corridor, that Linda's apartments were much the same.

The room in which they were presently standing far surpassed anything they had seen so far, however. Unfurnished, it would have made a reasonable ballroom; furnished, it resembled nothing so much as a room in the British Museum.

Though that was hardly fair, Beth admitted, aware that this salon was essentially Mediterranean in design. Although it possessed an abundance of old and evidently valued items, its high ceiling and Moorish arches were definitely created for a warmer climate.

And it had obviously been designed for entertaining, too. Between inlaid cabinets and bronze statuary, there were plenty of comfortable chairs and sofas, set about in groups to promote a sociable ambience. There were flowers, too, spilling from traditional Greek urns, and delicate occasional tables, on fragile, hand-carved stems.

But it was the vivid colours that impressed Beth most, colours picked out in embroidered cushions and jewel-bright carpets. The white walls were studded with pictures and icons which mirrored this brilliance. Even the flowers were rich and exotic, their bright, waxy petals like blood against the stone.

For, like all the Greek houses Beth had ever seen, the villa was built of stone, both for warmth and coolness. In winter, when the cold winds blew down from northern Europe, she guessed it would be warm and cosy, and now, in summer, its thick walls were a protection from the heat. It had surprised her that Alex's father hadn't had an air-conditioning system installed, but the villa had evidently been built before such refinements were available.

'Beautiful, isn't it?' she murmured in Linda's ear, and the younger woman gave her a wry look.

'If you like this sort of thing,' she conceded, wrapping her arms across her midriff, and giving the room only a cursory glance. 'Where do you think they are?'

'They?' Beth frowned. 'Oh, you mean Mr Thiarchos and his father.'

'Who else?' Linda spoke carelessly, but Beth knew she was not at all relaxed about this meeting.

'Well——' Beth trod across an exquisitely woven Turkish carpet '—maybe he hasn't come back yet. The older Mr Thiarchos, I mean. He could still be in Athens.'

It was her own wish, she realised, but Linda doused it. 'I heard a car,' she declared depressingly, following Beth across to the windows. Beyond the lamplit room, a flower-strewn courtyard was floodlit to reveal another tinkling fountain. 'Who else could it have been?' She shivered, as a huge moth threw itself at the glass. 'Ugh, I hate those things!'

'They're harmless enough,' said Beth reassuringly, wishing the moth were all they had to deal with. 'Look, it's pretty really. Can you see the colours in its wings?'

'Too well,' said Linda, pushing her hands into her trouser pockets and turning away. 'Oh, God! Why don't they come and get it over with?'

The sound of approaching footsteps had her freezing where she stood, however, and Beth automatically moved closer to her, although whether for Linda's sake or her own she couldn't be certain. In any event, they presented a united front as a man who couldn't be anyone else but Alex's father strode into the room. He wasn't as tall, and he was decidedly younger than she had expected, but his features were a broader—and perhaps a little swarthier—version of his son's.

'Ah, you are here!' he exclaimed, coming towards them with a smile on his lips and his hands outstretched. His eyes flickered briefly over Beth, before settling on the younger woman's face. 'You must be Linda,' he averred, and Linda, who had drawn her hands out of her pockets at his approach, had them taken in a determined clasp, and a kiss bestowed on either cheek. 'Welcome to Greece!'

'Thank you.' Linda's swallow was convulsive.

'It is my regret that you must come here in such unhappy circumstances,' he added, holding on to her hands, and searching her face with his dark compelling eyes. 'Please know that I share your grief.'

His sympathy didn't reach his eyes, Beth noticed, with a certain tightening of her stomach. She had the feeling that this whole charade was being enacted for someone else's benefit, and she was hardly surprised to see Alex

Thiarchos watching them from the arched doorway. Unlike his father, he was not wearing a dinner-jacket. As a concession to the heat, perhaps, he was wearing a loose silk shirt, and his dark skin contrasted sharply with the white fabric. His appearance never failed to disconcert her, and it took an actual effort to concentrate on what Linda was saying.

'You're very kind.'

Linda's voice trembled, and her nervousness was obvious. Beth guessed she had not expected this kind of a welcome from a man she had been led to believe had opposed her relationship with Tony, and she thought how clever it was of Constantine Thiarchos to take the initiative from her. Already, Linda was beginning to question the image she had formed of Tony's grandfather, and wonder whether the description she had been given of him had been totally unbiased.

'And you must be—Miss Haley.' No one could accuse Constantine Thiarchos of neglecting his manners, but Beth felt herself stiffening with instinctive dislike. It was hard to remember that this was her child's grandfather, too. A blood relation already, although he was unaware of it. 'It was thoughtful of you to give up your time to accompany my granddaughter-in-law. I am sure she appreciates your concern.' He paused. 'As I do, of course.'

But he didn't. Beth knew that, just as she knew he resented her being here. He was looking at her with cold grey eyes that were so like, yet unlike, his son's. He was letting her see his displeasure. What did he hope? That she'd turn around and leave? If only she could.

'I'm afraid it was your son's idea,' she declared coolly, not prepared to allow this man to think, even for a moment, that she had *wanted* to come here. Aware that Alex was watching her now, she gave an unconsciously defiant shrug of her shoulders. 'I hadn't planned on coming to Greece, Mr Thiarchos. It's a little hot for me at this time of the year. But how could I refuse?'

Constantine's mouth tightened. 'But surely, Miss Haley, an unexpected trip to the Levant cannot have been entirely unwelcome.'

'I didn't say it was unwelcome—just a little inconvenient, that's all,' she responded pleasantly, conscious now of Linda's horrified expression. 'I'm sure you understand, Mr Thiarchos.' She thought of his grandson's funeral that he hadn't attended. 'We can't always do what we want to do, can we?'

Constantine's lips thinned. 'Evidently not,' he conceded, in a harsh tone. Then, turning back to the less demanding needs of his daughter-in-law, he gestured towards the cabinet, which one of the servants had come in and opened during his altercation with Beth. 'Come, let me offer you an aperitif, my dear. A little retsina, maybe. Have you tried our local wine? It is flavoured with the resin from pine trees, you know.' He tipped his head from side to side. 'It is our best known vintage, but perhaps an acquired taste. We will see.'

Linda went with him willingly, evidently afraid that Beth might say something else to embarrass her, and Alex moved swiftly to take her place. 'Bravo,' he said, skimming the back of Beth's neck with a teasing finger. 'It's not often my father is forced to back down.'

Beth flinched at his touch. His lean fingers felt so possessive, somehow, and she was intensely conscious of his nearness. She could smell the soap he had used, mingling with the male scent of his body. And knew a crazy impulse to move closer to him, and the cynical protection he afforded.

'He didn't back down,' she contradicted him tautly, as eyes considerably warmer than his father's surveyed her heated face. 'He just decided not to pursue it, that's all. He was probably considering Linda's feelings.'

'My father doesn't consider anyone's feelings but his own,' retorted Alex softly. 'Don't underestimate yourself. The old man didn't like having his opinion questioned.'

'Then I probably shouldn't have done it,' said Beth uneasily, glancing across to where Linda was happily tasting the wine she had been given. 'This isn't my problem. Your father's right. I shouldn't be here.'

'I wanted you here.' Alex's breath fanned the pale skin exposed by the scoop neckline of her dress. 'Did I tell you, you look beautiful? You've put on a little weight. It suits you.'

Beth's breath faltered. 'Please——'

'Please what?' His eyes mocked her quivering confusion, and she had to force herself not to check the tightness of the dress. Behind her back, his hand slid possessively over the swell of her hips, trailing down to her thigh without his father's being aware of it. 'Do you have any idea what you do to me? God, when I'm with you, I feel like a raw youth, hot and——'

'Would you like to try the retsina, Miss Haley?'

Beth had never thought she would be glad to hear Constantine Thiarchos's voice, but she was. Moving jerkily perhaps, but determinedly just the same, she crossed the room to where Linda and her grandfather-in-law were standing. 'Um—perhaps. Just a little,' she agreed, shivering when Alex came to stand beside her. 'This—this is quite a place, Mr Thiarchos. Do you live here all year long?'

Constantine looked as if he was surprised by her friendly tone, but he was sufficiently diplomatic not to mention it. 'Whenever I can,' he conceded, handing her a glass of the strongly scented wine, and watching her taste it with a speculative eye. 'I have a house in Athens, of course, and in various other capitals of the world, where I can entertain, when necessary. But the Villa Vouliari is my home, my spiritual home, if you like. I was born here, Miss Haley, just as my father was before me. And my sons were born here, and their sons, too. Each succeeding generation. It is—what do you call it?— a tradition.'

'I see.'

For a moment, even the awareness of Alex's thigh, brushing the hem of her skirt, lost its threat. He was telling her that, for the last goodness knew how many years, every Thiarchos offspring had been born here. But not her child, she thought unsteadily. He didn't know it, but she was going to break the tradition.

'You don't approve, Miss Haley?'

He was intuitive. She'd give him that. Even that slight crack in her resistance had been noticed, and she knew she couldn't afford to make any mistakes while Constantine Thiarchos was around.

'On the contrary,' she replied, taking refuge behind her glass, and wishing she hadn't drawn attention to herself in that way. 'I think it sounds rather—feudal.'

'It is,' remarked Alex lazily, and his eyes probing the uncertainty of hers were blatantly sensual. But only she was aware of it, she thought wildly, struggling to regain the composure that seemed to have deserted her. 'My father likes to think he has the right of tenure over all our lives.' His head lifted. 'Isn't that right, Papa?'

Constantine's mouth thinned. 'I do not think Linda wishes to hear your opinion on this matter, Alexander.' He transferred his dark gaze to the young woman beside him. 'My son enjoys mocking me, my dear.'

'I wouldn't say that.' Alex's tone was less indulgent now. 'I'm merely warning my daughter-in-law of your tendency to try and control people, Papa.' He looked at Linda now. 'Like many predators, my father is most dangerous when he is being kind. Once he has found your weakness, beware!'

'Oh, Mr Thiarchos!'

It was obvious Linda hadn't the faintest idea how to respond to this, and Beth decided that, despite her own misgivings, she was glad she was here.

'I think you're exaggerating, Mr Thiarchos,' she declared, addressing herself to Alex deliberately. 'I'm sure your father isn't half as frightening as you're pretending. He seems fairly tame to me.' Which was throwing down the gauntlet with a vengeance, she thought apprehensively, but at least it diverted their attention from Linda.

And, as luck would have it, the maid appeared at that moment, to announce that their meal was waiting. Or, at least, that was Beth's interpretation of her words, confirmed by Constantine Thiarchos's proposal that they all adjourn to the dining salon. But his eyes flickered somewhat coldly over her pale face as he made the suggestion, and she guessed he would not forget what he would consider a thinly veiled insult.

The dining salon adjoined the living-room, another long, expansive room, with a huge refectory table, which looked as if it might once have served a monastery. It was heavily carved, and so solidly built that Beth imagined it would take a whole army of servants to move it. But tonight, set with shining silver and crystal, decorated with waxy white magnolias and trailing ferns, and lit by tall scented candles, it flouted any relevance to the past.

Because the table was so long, places had been set at only one end. Constantine Thiarchos occupied the high-backed chair at the end, of course, with Alex and Linda facing one another on his right and left hand respectively, and Beth facing an empty chair, a little further along. A less arrogant host might have arranged things differently, she reflected, a little drily, but she was the outsider here, and she wasn't going to be allowed to forget it.

The meal, however, was delicious. And although she hadn't expected to be able to eat anything Beth found herself emptying her plate. She was hungry, that was all, she told herself, as she swallowed the last morsel of the *souvlaki*, which was pork, spit-roasted, and served with savoury rice and vegetables. And perhaps she was eating to compensate for her nerves. It had nothing to do with her condition, she insisted, as she touched the faint swelling at her waist.

'Too much?'

Alex's lazy enquiry had her pressing guilty hands against her knees. 'I beg your——?'

'I thought you were feeling sick,' he broke in easily. 'You rubbed your stomach. Greek food can be a little rich for western European tastes.'

'Oh, no.'

Beth's face was flushed with colour, but at least Linda and his father didn't appear to have noticed. They were discussing the merits of the wine, and the fact that the Thiarchos corporation owned vineyards in another part of Attica. It seemed an innocuous conversation, but Beth had been wondering if Alex's warning had been so far-fetched, after all. For some reason, Constantine was endeavouring to gain the girl's confidence, and from what Beth could hear he was succeeding.

'You've eaten Greek food before?' Alex lifted his glass to the light, and Beth was briefly dazzled by the glow. 'I never asked. Have you been to Greece before?'

Beth swallowed. 'Once,' she conceded reluctantly, curiously loath to discuss anything about her past with him, and Alex frowned.

'When? Where did you stay?'

'It was years ago,' said Beth dismissively. 'When I was a child. We stayed in Thebes.'

'We?'

'My father and—and my sister and myself.'

'You have a sister?'

Beth took a breath. 'Not any more.'

'What do you mean, not any more?' Alex rested his elbows on the table and regarded her intently.

'She's dead,' said Beth shortly.

Alex frowned. 'An accident?'

'I—yes. Yes, an accident.'

Her hesitation was a mistake. 'Not an accident, then,' he interpreted correctly. 'She was ill?'

Beth sighed. 'If you must know, she died of an overdose.'

Alex's dark eyes widened. 'I see.'

'Do you?' Conversely, Beth wanted to tell him the truth now. 'My sister wasn't an addict, Mr Thiarchos. She was injured, badly injured, in a plane crash. She suffered a lot of pain before she died.' And not just physical pain, she added silently. Joy had lost more than her looks in those months before she died.

Alex lifted his shoulders now. 'I'm sorry.'

Beth bent her head. 'It happened a long time ago.'

'A long—but she was your sister!'

'We had different mothers,' said Beth unwillingly. 'Joy was twelve years older than me.'

'And how old were you when she died?'

Beth hesitated. 'Fifteen.'

Alex regarded her gently. 'But you still miss her.'

Unexpectedly, Beth felt the prick of tears behind her eyes. It was so long since she had spoken of Joy with anyone. Her father had spent the last years of his life too wrapped up in his own bitterness to care.

But it reminded her of her own sworn intention never to give any man that kind of hold over her, and, flicking a careless finger beneath her nose, she summoned a bright smile.

'Sometimes,' she said, with a look in her eyes that warned him not to pursue it. She lifted her glass to him in a mocking salute. 'To life, hmm? In all its endless variety!'

CHAPTER EIGHT

BETH sat on a cushioned stool at the mirrored dressing-table, slowly tugging a brush through her hair. The action of the bristles against her scalp always had a therapeutic effect, and the tight band that had encircled her temples when she first came into the room was gradually beginning to ease.

But it had not been an easy evening, she thought, leaning towards her reflection, to examine the pale blue shadows that had appeared beneath her eyes. What with keeping a surreptitious eye on Constantine Thiarchos on one hand, and parrying his son's remarks on the other, she felt as if she had suffered a baptism of fire.

And it wasn't nearly over yet. Linda had informed her, on their way to bed, that Tony's grandfather had suggested they stay for a week, not just the couple of days they had originally intended. His proposal was that Linda should take the opportunity to familiarise herself with the area, have an impromptu holiday, indeed. As well as getting to know the family better, she had added. Apparently, Alex's brother, George, and his wife, were due at the end of the week. Perhaps she owed it to Tony's memory to substantiate their marriage.

Which wasn't what she had said before she left England. But, when Beth attempted to remind her of that, Linda had revealed a totally unexpected side to her nature. 'You embarrassed me tonight,' she declared, hands balled into fists in her pockets, head thrown back to demonstrate her resentment. 'I don't know what you thought you were doing, practically accusing Tony's father of forcing you to come here! And arguing with Tony's grandfather over it. God, I didn't know where to look! These are my relations, Beth. I may not have wanted to meet them, but I certainly don't want to hurt them. Not when they've been so nice. And it was kind of them to let you come, too. I mean, they don't know you at all. I think you should appreciate it.'

Beth had said nothing. She couldn't. She knew if she had attempted to argue with Linda they probably would have had an all-out row, and she couldn't let that happen. All the same, it would be ironic if Linda asked her to leave, she thought bitterly. She wondered how the girl would feel if Beth told her the truth.

She sighed. Why was nothing ever simple? On the surface, she was here as Linda's friend, but, underneath that facile fact, lurked a whole glut of complications.

She stopped brushing her hair and let her hands fall into her lap. Several strands of blonde silk clung to the bristles of the brush, and she picked them off rather cynically. It was just as well her hair was so fair, she thought. She was sure she must have a score of grey hairs by now.

And, as she sat there, the silence of the room gathered around her. Distantly, she thought she could hear the murmur of the ocean, but within these four walls she felt chillingly alone. Which was silly really, she told herself, glancing about her. No one could have asked for a more attractive apartment, and the maid had come in, while they were at dinner, and turned down the bed for her.

It was like being in a hotel, she thought. Everything had been thought of. From the array of toiletries in the adjoining bathroom, to the crystal bottles of expensive perfume on the dressing-table, her every need had been anticipated. So wasn't it a pity she didn't appreciate it?

The room was lit by a number of lamps, including the concealed strip over the dressing-table. But now Beth turned them all out, except for the bronze-shaded onyx beside the bed, and walked on bare feet to the window. The long, silk-printed curtains had been closed by the maid earlier, and she drew the folds aside to peer out.

The hem of the curtain brushed her ankle and she shivered. The loosely tied robe was all she was wearing, and it had parted to expose her leg from heel to thigh. Her skin felt strangely sensitive this evening, and even the light touch of the raw fabric caused a delicate tightening of her nerve-endings. She felt tense, unsettled; as if even the warm air in the room was actually pressing against her flesh.

It was stupid, but she was more aware of herself in this place than she had ever been before. Her nipples were puckered against the cream satin of her robe, and the muscles of her thighs were taut and anxious. If it weren't such a ridiculous notion, she would have said her whole body ached, physically ached, and the need to escape the bands of her own frustration became an almost overwhelming force.

Dropping the curtain as if it burned her, she turned back into the room, crossing her arms at her midriff, and drying her damp palms on her sleeves. This was crazy, she told herself impatiently. It wasn't as if Alex Thiarchos had done anything to warrant such a response. On the contrary, he had been unexpectedly civil, and no one could have guessed from his attitude this evening that their relationship had ever been anything more than what it appeared.

Perhaps that was the trouble, she thought, with an unwilling burst of honesty. Perhaps she secretly enjoyed their confrontations, got a certain satisfaction from matching his barbed comments with her own. Life was certainly not dull when Alex was around, and perhaps she was disappointed that he hadn't made good on his threat.

But *no*!

The very idea that she might welcome another encounter with the man who had forced her to come here was ludicrous. Just because he had been half decent this evening was no reason to change her opinion of his behaviour. And both he and Linda had, in their own ways, implied that her presence here was superfluous. So what was stopping her from leaving in the morning?

Her mouth felt suddenly dry, and, going into the bathroom, she filled a glass with water and swallowed it down. But the dryness, like the fretful mood that was gripping her, was as much a psychological state as a physical one, and, setting down the glass, she walked back into the bedroom.

The curtains were still ajar, and although she went to close them the distant murmur of the ocean caught her imagination. Out there, beyond the gardens of the villa, the untamed beauty of the night was beckoning. Why didn't she take a walk, instead of moping about here? The exercise might tire her, and it would certainly chase any unwelcome feelings of promiscuity away.

It only took a few minutes to shed the satin robe in favour of a T-shirt and shorts. She chose dark colours— a plum-coloured T-shirt and burgundy shorts—deliberately. She had no desire for anyone to observe her leaving the villa. No desire for anyone to feel obliged to accompany her.

She let herself out of the French doors that opened on to the cloistered walkway outside her room. A pillared terrace encircled the inner courtyard of the villa, edged by a low stone wall, covered with flowering vines and wistaria.

It occurred to her, as she left the terrace, that she hadn't given any thought to the security arrangements at the villa. The two men she had seen on her arrival were unlikely to have gone off duty when it got dark. On the contrary, their numbers were likely to be supplemented with others, and maybe even a dog or two. Beth swallowed. The prospect of possibly meeting an angry Dobermann or Rottweiler almost had her heading back to the villa.

But common sense—or was it simple stubbornness?— kept her going. She couldn't believe there was any real danger in taking a walk by moonlight. And there was a moon, an almost full one, and it felt so good to be out in the cool night air.

All the same, she was a little surprised that she saw no one lurking in the shadows. There wasn't even the glow of a lighted cigarette to betray a watching presence. Well, perhaps body-guards didn't smoke these days. After all, her only experience of them had been gleaned from old black-and-white movies.

Beyond the courtyard, shallow steps revealed the existence of a swimming-pool. A swath of green water was underlit to display a mosaic of classic tiles, with Poseidon and Aphrodite sporting on its base. There was a row of white-painted cabanas, nestling in a grove of pines, and the roof of a shadowy bell-tower, arching above the trees.

Beyond the pool, the ground was terraced, with rose-hung pergolas, and the rich scent of broom. The sound of the ocean was much stronger here, and when her rubber-soled shoes slapped against rock she saw that she was immediately above the sandy cove.

She paused for a moment, taking huge breaths of the salted air. Apart from the muted roar of the ocean, and the whisper of a breeze through the pines, there was little sound. Athens, with its busy airport and hectic streets, might have been hundreds of miles away. Here, there was peace, and a heady sense of isolation.

She looked down, and saw the moonlight glinting on stone steps cut into the hillside. Evidently, that was how you reached the cove, she reflected. If the Thiarchoses' guests got bored with the pool, they could go and swim in the ocean. The cove was totally private, as she had seen on their arrival.

She hadn't intended to go down to the beach. Already, her legs were aching with the effort of balancing herself against the curve of the downward slope, and she was tired. It had been a long day, physically and mentally, and she thought she might sleep now that her restlessness had been blunted.

But, as she stood there, gazing dreamily towards the water, she saw something moving in the shallows. She'd probably have thought nothing of it, if she hadn't had that earlier awareness of a curious absence of security. She'd have assumed it was the shift of the moonlight, or her eyes playing tricks with her. Not tried to identify it, with an intensity born of fear.

It was a man. She was almost sure of it. Someone was down there, in the water; someone dark and sleek, with an absence of angles. Someone who might be wearing a wet-suit.

But who? And what ought she to do? She wished now she had seen one of the security guards. Even in her broken Greek, she was sure she could have made him understand.

And then the man stood up, and her breath caught in her throat. Like some Greek god rising from the waves, he trod through the shallows and on to the beach. With his arms raised to squeeze the water from his hair, over-long hair, which clung damply to the back of his neck, his identity was unmistakable. It was Alex Thiarchos who had been swimming; Alex Thiarchos she had glimpsed in the water; Alex Thiarchos, who strode out on to the sand, lean, and muscled, and totally naked.

Beth exhaled shakily. She had never seen a man naked before, not like this, so naturally, and so careless that anyone might see him. That night at the flat—God! She could hardly remember how he had looked then!—was like another time, another world. She had been so afraid of doing something wrong, or letting him see how scared she really was. She supposed she had looked at his body; she certainly had touched it. But all she really remembered were the feelings he had aroused; the wild and frightening loss of all control.

Her breath quivered, and with it came an awarenesses of how she was feeling now. The needs she had suppressed in her bedroom earlier, the desperate needs that had driven her to take this walk in the moonlight, had all been rekindled. What price now the peace and seclusion she had thought she was seeking? The unashamed sight of Alex Thiarchos's body had shown her just how artificial they had been.

An aching feeling was invading her lower limbs, a strange weakness, which was magnified a hundredfold when he bent and picked up his towel and started to dry himself. Yet still she lingered, held by an emotion that was as old as time itself. Curiosity, and the forbidden pleasure of watching him without his being aware of it, kept her where she was, and shivers of anticipation ran down her legs when he abraded his chest and thighs.

God, she would like to do that, she thought wildly. She would like to tangle her fingers in the fine hair that gathered between his pectoral muscles and ran, like a dark arrow, down between his legs. Her fingers itched to touch him, to caress his shoulders, and smooth his biceps, to glide over his abdomen, and shape his sex . . .

Her breath hissed out in an unsteady sigh, and she felt an unfamiliar dampness between her thighs. Dear God, she thought incredulously, as a haze of longing closed her eyes for a moment, she was becoming aroused. If Alex climbed the steps now, and took her in his arms, there wouldn't be a thing she could do about it. Or want to, she admitted chillingly. What had begun as a seemingly foolproof exercise was rapidly deteriorating into chaos. It was hard to remember now how detached she had felt when she devised it. She had been so convinced that she wouldn't get hurt, that she *couldn't* get hurt, but she was wrong. It seemed as if she wasn't so different from her mother and her sister, after all.

But she had to be, she told herself savagely. Any interest Alex Thiarchos had in her was purely physical. If he was attracted to her, and she thought perhaps he might be, it was because of how she looked and nothing else.

And she knew, better than anyone, how superficial that could be. Her mother's beauty had led her into numerous affairs that had broken her husband's heart. The fact that she had died in a freak skiing accident, when

Beth was only eight years old, had not eased her husband's pain. And Joy's death only seven years later had ensured that her younger sister learned the lesson well. Joy had been a successful model, before she was injured in the plane crash. But the man she loved, the man she had been going to marry, had not been able to cope with the facial scarring she had suffered...

Now Beth opened her eyes again, eyes that had grown moist with the grief she still felt for her sister, and cast a final glance at the beach. At least thinking about Joy had dispelled the awful weakness in her knees. She would go to bed, and put all thoughts of Alex Thiarchos, and his sexy body, out of her head.

But the beach was empty. She blinked rapidly, half convinced that her tears must be blinding her, but even after she had rubbed the heels of her hands across her eyes the image remained the same. There was no one there. The beach was deserted. And, although she looked up and down the stretch of moon-silvered sand, she could see no evidence of anyone's occupancy.

Had she dreamed it? she wondered. Had her own frustrated emotions conjured up the substance of the man? She'd only closed her eyes for a few moments. He couldn't have disappeared. It wasn't possible.

Yet he wasn't there. That much was indisputable. Even the sand where he had been standing looked smooth and undisturbed. Of course, she couldn't see it clearly from this angle, and perhaps the tide was coming in, but it certainly looked like it. Like a mirage in the desert, he had vanished into the night.

And once again she was as nervy and on-edge as she had been before. The brief respite that thinking of Joy had given her might never have been. Where was he? she demanded silently, glancing half apprehensively about her. Why had he done this to her? He *had* been there. She knew it. She wouldn't sleep until she'd proved it.

With a feeling, half of impatience, half of dread, she started down the stone stairs. She was just going to the bottom of the steps, she told herself. Just to make sure she hadn't been dreaming. She refused to consider what she might do if her conviction proved groundless. She was sure now that there was another way up from the beach and he had used it.

The sand was quite firm beneath her soles, and she guessed that at high tide the water came fairly close to the cliffs. Uncomfortably close, she thought, reluctant to move away from the steps. She would hate to get trapped down here. Particularly when there didn't seem to be any other way of getting out.

'Looking for me?'

The voice came from behind her, and Beth's legs almost gave out on her. For all her suspicions, she had thought the cove was empty, and when Alex spoke to her she let out a little cry.

'Well, what else was I supposed to think?' he continued, moving away from the shadow of the rocks and emerging into the silvery light. 'You have been watching me for the past fifteen minutes, haven't you?' One dark eyebrow quirked. 'Do I take it that you liked what you saw?'

Beth sucked in her breath. It was difficult to think of anything to say, with him standing there watching her like a sphinx. Her only relief came from the fact that he had draped the towel around his hips to protect his modesty. Though, remembering how he had been acting earlier, she guessed it was more her feelings he was protecting than his own.

'I—don't know what you mean,' she got out at last, and knew herself for a hypocrite when she saw his mocking mouth. 'I—I was just going for a walk, that's all. I—I couldn't sleep.'

'Nor could I,' remarked Alex at last, evidently prepared to give her a little leeway. 'That's why I went for a swim. The water's so beautiful at this time of night.'

'I'm—sure.' Beth swallowed. 'Is—is it warm?'

'Why don't you find out?' he suggested softly. 'Just take off your clothes and help yourself.'

Beth gasped. 'I couldn't.'

'Why couldn't you?'

'Well, I—I don't—I'm not—wearing a bathing suit.'

'So?' His eyes darkened as they skimmed the taut curve of her breasts, and she prayed she was displaying no other signs of her arousal. 'The beach is private. There's no one else about.'

'You—you're about,' she declared huskily, and he grinned.

'So I am. But we've got nothing to hide from one another, have we, Beth?' He let go of the towel and let it fall to the sand. 'Come on. What have you got to lose?'

Beth turned her head away. 'You're—shameful!'

'*Shameless*,' amended Alex, putting out a hand, and cupping the sensitive nape of her neck. 'Beth—what are you afraid of? You followed me here, remember? Not the other way about.'

'I didn't follow——'

'All right, all right!' He raised his hands in a gesture of defeat. 'So you didn't follow me. You just came to find me, right?'

'No——' Beth turned to look indignantly at him, and then looked quickly away again. 'All right, I did see you from the top of the steps. But when I looked again you'd disappeared.'

'When you looked *again*?' Alex sounded perplexed. 'Funny, I thought you saw me cross to the steps. I was about to come up, when you started coming down.'

'Well, I didn't see you,' said Beth crossly, and Alex shrugged.

'You didn't move.'

'I'd—closed my eyes.' Beth gave him another fleeting glance. 'I—I was thinking about my sister. I don't care if you believe me or not. It's the truth.'

Alex studied her bent head. 'So—why did you come down?'

Beth made a dismissive gesture. 'No reason.'

'Oh, come on.' Alex lifted a silky strand of her hair and drew it across her mouth. 'You were curious where I'd gone. Admit it. You were looking for me. I think— I think you were wanting me just as much as I was wanting you.'

'No!'

Beth's denial was swift and indignant, but when his hands reached to cup her face she couldn't pull away. She felt mesmerised by his touch, and although his mouth merely brushed hers she had to steel herself not to lean into him.

'Sweet,' he breathed, against her lips. '*Theos,* Beth, where have you been all these years?'

Beth panicked. She couldn't let this happen again. She couldn't let him do this to her. Hadn't she just spent the last half-hour fretting over the fact that seeing him again had awakened all those half-forgotten feelings? Hadn't she proved her vulnerability by coming down here, by watching him, and letting his arrant sensuality stir emotions she had once fooled herself she could control? She had to stop him; now; before she repeated the madness.

She lifted her hands to his throat, and although the temptation to slip them around his neck was paramount she balled her fists and pressed him away. 'Let me go,' she demanded, her voice high and desperate, and she was hardly aware that he had offered no resistance until she was fleeing across the sand.

But, of course, she was going the wrong way. All that was ahead of her was the ocean, creeping up the beach now, as the tide turned. The steps—and escape—were behind her. As he had known when he let her get away from him, she thought bitterly. Oh, God! Why had she been such a fool?

She glanced round, fully expecting him to have followed her, but he hadn't. To her surprise, she saw he was standing at the foot of the steps now, his towel draped around his throat, and a pair of cut-off denims covering his hips from waist to knee.

Immediately, she felt even more of a fool. What had she expected? That he would chase her across the beach, and throw her down on to the sand? Had she really thought he might take her here, in full view of any other insomniac like herself? She had evidently been reading too many romantic novels. Such obvious melodrama was not for a man like Alex Thiarchos.

He seemed to be waiting for her, and, hunching her shoulders, she trudged back across the sand. What else could she do? she thought broodingly. She had acted like a schoolgirl, and it was up to her now to try and redress the balance.

'Ready?' he asked, when she reached him, and she nodded her head rather sulkily. 'OK.' He stepped away from the stairs. 'You go first. I'll follow.'

Beth couldn't have said 'thanks' to save her life. Everything: the walk, her uncharacteristic voyeurism, the feelings he had engendered, and her panic-stricken rejection of his lovemaking, seemed so ridiculous somehow. What was she afraid of, for God's sake? She had had sex with this man, hadn't she? What more could he do to her? He must think she was totally stupid.

And, perhaps because she wasn't paying as much attention to where she was going as she should have, her foot slipped. The sand had been damp, she remembered, and the soles of her shoes had lost much of their purchase on the smooth rocks. In consequence, although she tried to save herself, she stumbled backwards into Alex.

She heard his swift intake of breath as he attempted to save both of them, but the pull of gravity was too great. Or perhaps he didn't try hard enough, she thought later, when her blood had had time to cool, and she could think about it rationally. At any rate, they were only a couple of steps up from the beach, and the distance was not great.

To Beth, it all seemed to happen in slow motion. One moment, she was thinking of nothing but reaching the top of the steps, and putting as much space between herself and Alex as possible, and the next, she was falling through the air. She didn't worry about herself, or the baby, which was strange considering the freeze-frame motion of her fall. Her most immediate concern was that Alex was beneath her, and her greatest fear was that she might hurt him.

In the event, she did land on top of him, practically knocking all the air out of his lungs. But he was in better shape than most men of his age and profession, and the taut muscles of his midriff cushioned her fall without much damage to himself.

His only response was a rueful grunt, and by the time Beth had gathered herself sufficiently to roll off him his eyes were open wide and bright with amusement. 'Hey, I wanted you to fall for me, but not like this,' he teased, his eyes narrowing when he saw her consternation. 'You're not hurt, are you? I'm sorry I couldn't keep my balance.'

'It wasn't your fault,' said Beth hurriedly, struggling on to her knees. She lifted her hand, and swept one side of her hair back behind her ear. 'It was me. I wasn't thinking what I was doing. Are you all right?'

'Going to give me the kiss of life?' he suggested lazily, and then, aware of her very real concern, he shifted his shoulders against the sand. 'I seem to be still in one piece,' he assured her. 'Just a little winded, that's all. How about you?'

She shrugged, becoming aware that her hands were still resting on his forearm, and that his skin felt faintly damp and cool to the touch. And, as her eyes slid away from the low waistband of his cut-offs, and moved over his upper body, she saw little runnels of water from his still wet hair leaching away across his chest.

Her tongue sought her lips, almost without her being aware of it, as she anticipated what it could be like to taste that salt-laden moisture. She guessed it would taste of him, too, and her breath quickened at the idea of such an intimate act. God, she wondered, why did she have such thoughts about him? He didn't have to do anything. Her senses just seemed to take over.

'You didn't answer me,' he reminded her now, lifting his hand to cup the nape of her neck. 'Beth,' his voice had thickened, 'don't look at me like that. I'm trying to play this your way, but you don't make it very easy.'

'I—why—I don't know what you mean,' she stumbled, but the awareness of his hand under her hair was tying up her tongue. 'I haven't hurt myself, if that's what you mean.' She swallowed convulsively. 'Let—let me help you to get up. Goodness knows what anyone would think if they could see us.'

'No one will see us,' replied Alex huskily, his thumb moving in a circular movement behind her ear. 'I told the security guy to get lost while I had my swim. He won't come back, unless I call him.' He checked his hip pocket with his free hand. 'Providing I haven't smashed the phone.'

Beth moistened her lips. 'You've—got—a phone?'

It was a mindless thing to say in the present circumstances, but her brain couldn't cope with what was happening. The nearness of his flesh, the scent of the ocean on his skin, the musky fragrance of his body were all acting like triggers to her overwhelming awareness of his near-nakedness. Although she knew she ought to get away from him, and as quickly as possible, her body seemed to have a will of its own. Almost instinctively, she was leaning closer to him, fully aware that her T-shirt was no barrier to the burgeoning fullness of her breasts.

'Yeah, I've got a phone,' he answered her, and she knew he was only giving her careless question a mocking response. His thumb probed her ear. 'What to see it?'

Beth's breathing constricted. 'I—don't think so.'

'Why not?'

'Alex——'

'Hey, you remember my name!'

'Alex—we have to go back.'

'I'm not stopping you, am I?'

And he wasn't. Only she didn't seem capable of acting rationally. With his eyes on her, all she could think about was the spot where her knees were wedged against the warming skin of his midriff. And, when she did try to break the contact and stretch her legs, her toes brushed sensuously along his leg from thigh to knee.

She told herself it wasn't a deliberate provocation, but when Alex's hand moved to grip her wrist she knew she had gone too far. 'What are you trying to do to me?' he demanded, jerking her towards him, and the hand that had been gripping her neck slid possessively into her hair. His hand guided her lips to his with unerring accuracy, and when his hot breath invaded her mouth she knew she was not going to have the will to resist him. Besides, with the damp heat of his chest beneath her breasts, and the tentative awareness of his maleness just inches from her thigh, she couldn't really say that she wanted to. With his arms around her, and his hand moving sensually up and down her spine, she found her strongest impulse was to press herself against him, to ease the ache in her breasts, and assuage the need between her legs.

She felt her T-shirt come free of her shorts, and his hand slip beneath the cloth to spread against the yielding curve of her spine, and heard his strangled breath. 'Ah, God, Beth,' he groaned, rolling over with her, so that she was on her back now, and he was on top of her. 'Why in the name of heaven do you fight this? You know you want me, and God knows I want you, too. There are better places for this, I know, but right now it doesn't seem to matter.'

His mouth sought hers again then, hard and impassioned. His tongue slipped between her teeth, seeking a closer union—and found it in the darting inexperience of her response. She was trembling, but her senses felt as if they were on fire; a burning conflagration that threatened to consume her.

His eyes weren't lazy now. As he lifted his head to watch his strong fingers peel the T-shirt from her body, she saw their dusky glitter. With one hand, he traced a path from her shoulder to the swollen tip of her breast, then bent his head to nip the flesh before taking it into his mouth.

A sob rose in Beth's throat, and her palpitating heart beat wildly against her ribcage. Her senses felt as if they were swimming in a haze of mindless dark liquid, and her movements were slow and lethargic, yet furiously intent.

His hands moved down her body, exploring the curve of her waist, before sliding beneath the elasticated waistband of her shorts to cup her quivering bottom. His fingers touched the moist cleft, which jerked spasmodically beneath his touch, and then probed between her legs to find the wet heat of her arousal.

'Oh, God, Alex!' she gasped, unable to stay silent when he was doing such things to her, and the tight smile he gave her revealed his own compulsive involvement. When he rubbed himself against her, he was feeding his own need as well as hers, and the hard thrust of his manhood was hot against her stomach.

'Why the hell did you let me put these things on?' he demanded huskily, fighting feverishly to free himself from the close-fitting denim. The zip jammed, and he swore when he caught his finger on the metal teeth. But then they were off, and so were her shorts, and the muscled weight of his body pressed possessively against hers.

'Oh, that's good,' he groaned, content just for a moment to lie against her, and with an instinct she hardly knew she possessed Beth eased her hand between them to touch him. The hot, pulsating length of him was amazingly soft and velvety, and her thumb probed the moist tip in innocent exploration.

His intake of breath was convulsive, and the hand that moved to close over hers was shaky. 'God, Beth,' he said, through parched lips, 'don't do that!'

Beth frowned. 'I'm sorry——'

'Don't be,' he broke in weakly, and his mouth now was rueful and faintly mocking. 'It isn't that I don't like it. Just—too much, hmm? Right now, I don't have a lot of control.'

Beth's tongue touched her upper lip. 'I thought——'

'Yes. I can guess what you thought,' he agreed, evenly. He levered himself up to look down at her. 'You have no idea what you do to me, do you? I can't keep my hands off you.'

'No?'

It was just a whisper, and he repeated it as he bent to cover her mouth with his. Then, with infinite control, he parted her legs and eased himself into her, and the sigh he uttered was echoed in her soul.

It was so good to feel him there; in her; a part of her; healing that empty space inside her, which only he could fill. Dear God, how could she even pretend she didn't want him, when every nerve in her body was crying out for the release only he could give her?

His hands were moulding her, caressing her, and everywhere his hands touched his mouth followed. And slowly, but insistently, he began to move. His withdrawal from her body was the most delicate kind of torture, but just when her nails were digging into his shoulders, begging him not to leave her, he buried himself even deeper inside her. He spread her quivering muscles with his fullness, stretching her to the limits of her endurance, and then did it all over again.

She was hardly aware of him quickening his movements. Her whole being was focused on that pleasure-pain flowering inside her, that aching sweetness, which threatened her sanity and promised so much. And when he lifted himself on his elbows so that he could watch the place where his maleness joined him to her she lost what little control she had. She clutched his neck with nerveless fingers, bringing his eyes back to hers, and he let her draw him down to her, and wind her legs about him.

After that, there was no time to think of anything but him. Hunger and fever and need took hold of her, and the eager rocking motion of their bodies brought them both to that pinnacle of ecstasy Beth had been so sure she must have exaggerated. But she hadn't. As the spiralling thermals of passion took her higher and higher, she cried aloud with the wonder of it all. And Alex joined her as he reached his own climax, shuddering in her arms long after the spurting heat of his release had spilled inside her...

CHAPTER NINE

BETH awakened the next morning feeling dry-mouthed and slightly headachy. She felt as if she had slept too soundly and too long, but, looking at the clock on the bedside table, she knew that couldn't be the reason. It was barely half-past seven, and she hadn't tumbled into bed until after two o'clock.

And she knew why, knew it instantly, the moment her eyes opened on that sunlit Greek bedroom. She didn't need to see the brilliance of the sun, slanting through the blinds, and glinting on the jewelled icon that hung on the wall at the foot of her bed. She didn't need to hear the cicadas, or smell the fragrance of the thyme that grew wild on the cliffs, above the cove. She knew it with her body, knew it instinctively, and viscerally; in the tenderness of her breasts; in the slight ache that was present in her thighs; and in the faint soreness that throbbed between her legs. Knew it by the lingering sense of well-being—that vanished as soon as she sat up and felt the nausea rising in her throat.

She only just made it to the bathroom basin, and by the time she lifted her head all that was left of those early morning feelings was the dry mouth and the headache. She felt and looked like death, and she took a cold facecloth and pressed it against her moist forehead.

The coolness was a blessing, and as the nausea faded she actually found she was hungry. For a moment, she had had the awful suspicion that last night's excesses had been too much for a woman in her condition. It was weeks since she had actually vomited in the mornings, though she did still get occasional bouts of sickness during the day.

All the same, it was lucky she hadn't allowed Alex to accompany her back to her room. He had wanted to. And goodness knew, last night she had wanted him to as well. The idea of making love in a bed had been very appealing after making love on the sand. All right, Alex had dragged his towel beneath them, but her hair had got all gritty just the same. Afterwards, she had let him carry her into the water, and they had swum together, and made love together in the ocean. But she had drawn the line at their sleeping together.

'What would Linda think if she found out?' she had protested, and, although Alex had maintained he didn't give a damn what his daughter-in-law thought about their behaviour, he had eventually given in and let her have her way.

For which she would be eternally grateful, Beth thought this morning, giving thanks for whatever shred of sanity had compelled her to deny him. Apart from anything else, he couldn't be allowed to see her in broad daylight. She had slept naked, climbing nervelessly into bed and falling asleep almost immediately, so that now the thickening shape of her waistline was clearly visible. The rest of her body was so slim, she thought, turning sideways to view herself in the long mirrors. The curving swell of her stomach was definitely noticeable. Even her breasts looked fuller and heavier, the faint blue veins showing more prominently, the nipples a darker brown.

If she had had any doubts about her condition, and of course she hadn't, her appearance alone would have convinced her. And anyone else, she admitted ruefully. Her body was changing, not just inside, but out, and pretty soon she wouldn't be able to hide it, however ingeniously she might try.

She heard the knock on her bedroom door as she was brushing her teeth and panic gripped her. Dear God, what if it was Alex? What if he thought last night had given him the right to invade her space whenever he chose? She needed time to think before she saw him again. Time to assimilate what she was going to do, what she *could* do, without threatening the independence she had worked so hard to achieve.

'Beth! Beth, where are you?'

Linda's voice was both a jolt and a reprieve. At least it wasn't Alex, Beth consoled herself, snatching a velvety soft bath-sheet from the rack, and wrapping it about her. With luck, Linda wouldn't expect her to disrobe in front of her this morning. Without even the satin folds of the teddy to protect her, she felt exposed and vulnerable.

'I'm here,' she called now, coming to the door of the bathroom. She forced a smile. 'Good morning. You're up early.'

'I know.' Linda was hovering in the doorway to the corridor, and seemed to have forgotten her irritability of the night before. 'I couldn't sleep, so I went exploring. Do you know, there's a swimming pool? Mr Thiarchos was there. Tony's dad, that is. He was swimming, and when he saw me he invited me to join him. They have all sorts of swimwear in the cabanas there.' She grimaced. 'But no hairdriers, unfortunately. That's why my hair's still damp.'

'I see.' Beth felt an unwelcome spurt of envy. But she wasn't jealous, she assured herself. It was the idea of Linda sharing Alex's confidence that filled her with unease. 'He must be an early riser, too.'

'Mmm.' Linda nodded, pushing her hands into the hip pockets of her jeans, and arching her spine. 'Did—er—did you sleep well?'

'Oh—reasonably.' Beth lifted the hem of the towel and pretended to be wiping beads of moisture from her cheeks. She hoped Linda would think the abrasion was responsible for the unwilling colour that had stained her face at the girl's words, but it didn't prevent the rush of impatience she had felt at herself. *Blushing*! she chided. At her age! What on earth was happening to her?

'Are you sure?' Linda asked now, staring at her rather intently. 'I've just noticed you do look rather feverish. Are you running a temperature?'

'Of course not.' Beth managed a light laugh. 'I've just got up, that's all. I haven't even had a wash yet.'

'Oh.' Linda seemed to accept her explanation. 'Well, I'm glad, because Mr Thiarchos has suggested taking us out this morning. He says he wants to show us a little of the area. Temples; villages; vineyards. You know the sort of thing.'

'Ah——' Beth moistened her lips. 'Well, I'm sure you'll enjoy it, Linda. This is one of the most enchanting areas of Attica, and naturally Mr Thiarchos will know it like the back of his hand. He—he told me— at dinner last evening,' she inserted hastily, 'that he spent most of his youth here.'

'Yes, I know.' Linda nodded now. 'And you heard his father say that Tony was born here, too. Tony was an only child, you know. Isn't that sad?'

'Mmm.' Beth wondered why that news should give her any sense of reassurance. 'So—what time are you leaving?'

'Not me—*us*,' said Linda, reddening herself now. 'You're invited too, of course.'

'Oh, no.' Beth was adamant. 'Honestly. It's very kind of you to think of me, but, as you said last night, I'm really only here as your companion. You don't have to entertain me. I'd just as soon spend the morning—on— on the beach.' The beach was the last place she wanted to be, but Linda wasn't to know that. And, hoping that was the end of it, she offered the girl a friendly smile. 'And now, if you'll excuse me, I'm going to have a shower.'

'Wait!' Linda took a couple of steps forward, and Beth, who had been retreating into the bathroom, was forced to stop. 'About last night,' said Linda uncomfortably. 'I didn't mean what I said. About—about you embarrassing me, and all. I think I must have had too much wine or something. Of course you're entitled to your opinions. And—and I am grateful that you persuaded me to come.'

'Linda——'

'That's why you have to come out with us this morning.'

'I don't think so.'

'You must.' Linda looked desperate. 'Mr—Mr Thiarchos was most insistent that you should join us. I—I think he likes you. He was asking me all sorts of questions about you.'

'Really?' Beth spoke round the aridity of her throat. 'I—don't think I like the sound of that.'

'Oh, don't be silly.' Linda made an impatient sound. 'It was all perfectly innocent. He was just interested in your work, and what you do in your spare time. I told him how good you are at your job and that you're taking a year off to write a book. He was really interested in that.'

Beth felt the colour drain out of her face. Dear God, she thought, she was going to faint again. As she had almost done that day at Linda's foster mother's home. But she mustn't. She *mustn't*. Her behaviour had aroused far too many suspicions as it was, and if Alex should decide to call a doctor——

'Are you sure you're all right?'

Linda was watching her closely again, and with a superhuman effort Beth pulled herself together. 'I'm fine,' she declared, though she clearly wasn't. And then, because the twin horrors of having to justify her absence to Alex, and of him spending the whole morning quizzing Linda, were simply too awful to anticipate, she gave in. 'And—please thank Mr Thiarchos for his invitation, will you? Tell him I will join you, after all.' She grimaced, though not for the reasons Linda imagined. 'After—after I've had my shower.'

A maid had been in her absence, and when Beth returned to the bedroom it was to find a tray of coffee and hot rolls steaming on the table by the long windows. There was also milk, and cream, strongly flavoured butter, and a thick and juicy conserve, and a tall glass of freshly squeezed orange juice, which tasted as if the fruit had just been plucked that morning.

Beth attacked the meal with real enthusiasm. Hunger seemed to be her greatest problem at the moment, and she always felt better after a good breakfast. For someone who, for years, had existed on toast and coffee, she found she had an inordinately large appetite. Which was something else she would have to watch.

Nevertheless, she ate everything on the tray, gambling that Alex and his father were unlikely to question the servants about their guests' preferences. And it was delicious. Even the coffee—Continental, not Greek—was very acceptable, and she lay back in her chair afterwards, wishing she could just relax for a while.

But the knowledge that Linda was becoming far too familiar with her father-in-law soon had her rummaging through her suitcase, looking for a satisfactory outfit. She had deliberately not brought a bathing suit with her, working on the premise that without a swimsuit she couldn't be expected to swim. The fact that she had swum, and without a swimsuit at that, was incidental. That had been at night, and not even Alex could expect her to go skinny-dipping in broad daylight. And then she remembered what Linda has said about her own swim that morning, and her apprehensions returned anew.

She chose shorts now. Worn with a hip-length tunic, whose pleated style would have concealed a longer-term pregnancy than she could boast, they were both practical and flattering. The tunic's primary colour was a pale primrose-yellow, with panels of dark navy that were repeated in the piping that edged the collarless neckline and hem, and in the narrow-legged Bermudas. Her arms were bare and they seemed very white when compared to Alex's brown skin.

But she wasn't going to think about Alex, she told herself, as she laced her canvas boots and ran a final brush through her hair. She had to deal with him, and that was that. She couldn't spend every minute of the day in her room.

She thought about leaving the room as she had done the night before, by the French doors, and walking along the vine-hung colonnade. But it wouldn't do to appear too familiar with her surroundings, and after collecting her sunglasses she chose the corridor instead. Closing her door, she walked the not inconsiderable distance to the cool airiness of the entrance hall.

And, although she had steeled herself for her first meeting with Alex, she was almost disappointed when she found he wasn't there. The large room where they had gathered the night before was empty, and she was wondering what she ought to do when Constantine Thiarchos appeared at the open windows. He had evidently been in the courtyard, and she thought how lucky it was that she hadn't chosen that route herself.

'Ah, *kalimera*, Miss Haley,' he greeted her formally. 'How are you this morning?'

'Um—very well, thank you.' Beth held up her head. 'It's another lovely morning, isn't it?' She looked beyond him, into the sunlit courtyard. 'This is such a beautiful place.'

'I am so glad you like it.' Constantine came further into the room. He was dressed all in white this morning: white shirt; white trousers; even white shoes, she saw with some amusement. Was it a conscious effort to deny the darker shades of his personality? 'Did you sleep well?'

Now why did she feel as if that was a loaded question? she wondered uneasily. Linda had asked her the same question, and she hadn't felt any undercurrents with her.

'I—yes. Yes, very well, thank you,' she conceded tautly. 'My room is very comfortable.'

'Is it?' Once again, she had the feeling that he was baiting her. 'You did not find it too hot or unfamiliar?'

'N-o.' But Beth had the distinct impression that Alex's father knew she was not being absolutely truthful. 'I—went out like a light.'

'Like a light?' He frowned now. 'What is this? Like a light? You had trouble with the lamps in your room?'

'No.' Beth wished she hadn't elaborated now. 'I just meant—I fell asleep as soon as my head touched the pillow.'

'I see.' But he clearly wasn't convinced. 'Well, you must get my staff to show you the grounds of the villa today. And the cove, of course. There are steps leading down to the cove. It is completely private, you know.'

And that was when she knew. Knew for certain that Constantine Thiarchos knew of her walk the night before. Probably knew where she had gone, as well, she thought sickly. Oh, God, had he had his security guards watching them all the time?

She knew she had to say something; anything, to fill the pregnant silence that had fallen. A *pregnant* silence! she reflected mockingly. Oh, that was rich! Even her thoughts were betraying her. What must this man be thinking?

'Thank you.' The polite words of gratitude were probably not what he had expected after her plain speaking of the night before, but she was in no state to face another argument with him. Besides, whatever she said, he would only believe what he chose to believe. And, whether or not she had planned that meeting with Alex, what had happened had certainly seemed no coincidence.

'I—understand—my son is taking you and Linda for a drive this morning,' Constantine went on, after a moment. 'Forgive me, but does it not seem more appropriate that Alex should have some time alone with his daughter-in-law? I myself would offer to entertain you if I could, but regrettably I must spend the day in Athens. Nevertheless, the grounds of the villa are at your disposal.'

Beth's face flamed. 'I was more than willing to forgo the outing, Mr Thiarchos,' she declared stiffly, 'but your son insisted on my accompanying them.'

'Yes. Well, Alex is apt to be—how shall I say?—a little indiscreet at times, Miss Haley. He does not always think before he acts. I am sure if you insisted he would not force you to attend.'

Beth had never felt so humiliated. No wonder Constantine's competitors in the business world regarded him with such suspicion. He was completely single-minded; completely ruthless. He didn't want her here, and whatever had happened between her and Alex he was determined to keep her in her place.

'I——' Words failed her. How could she compete with someone who would use any means at his disposal to achieve his ends? 'Um—Linda—won't go without me,' she finished lamely.

'Linda will do as——'

She's told! The words hovered in the air between them, eloquent, but unspoken, and with the sixth sense she always felt around Alex Beth looked behind her.

And she was hardly surprised to see him there, his shoulder propped against the door-jamb, a lazy smile lifting the corners of his mouth, but hardly penetrating the sombre darkness of his eyes. In a black collarless shirt, whose sleeves were turned back over his hair-roughened forearms, and black chinos, he looked achingly familiar, and, for all her earlier misgivings, she was desperately glad to see him.

But, before she could reach past the shivering awareness of the previous night's intimacy and say so, his father intervened. 'Ah, Alex,' he said jovially, as if Beth hadn't just been the recipient of the cutting edge of his tongue, 'I was just telling our guest she must see more of the villa today. Did you know we have a swimming-pool, Miss Haley? And tennis courts, too. Perhaps my secretary, Spiro, could be persuaded to give you a game if——'

'I know what you were telling Miss Haley, Papa.' Alex's voice broke into his father's speech without obvious expression. He came into the room as he spoke, and tucked his thumbs into the back of the belt that hung low on his hips. 'I think I should make something clear, here and now: Beth is my guest, not yours.'

Constantine's nostrils flared. 'But this is my house!' he retorted, before lapsing into a spate of Greek that was incomprehensible to anyone with only a cursory knowledge of the language.

But Beth could guess what he was saying. It was obvious by the glances he cast in her direction, and the fulminating anger of his words. She turned away in dismay, unwilling to appear even remotely interested in their exchange, and thought how naïve she had been in coming here. Where was the frail patriarch she had painted for Linda before they left England? This infuriated little man was no grief-stricken grandparent. He was hard, and unforgiving, and certainly capable of writing those letters that Linda had told her about.

But, before she could move away, Alex reached out and linked his fingers loosely round her wrist. 'Stay,' he said, when she turned incredulous eyes in his direction. And then, to his father, 'Speak English, Papa. Beth only speaks a little of our language as yet. But——' he looked at her again, and she felt her bones melting at the expression in his eyes '—she'll learn. I'll teach her myself.'

Constantine said something under his breath which she was sure wasn't very complimentary, but a warning glance from his son had him clenching his lips. Nevertheless, he couldn't resist one final salvo. 'You are a fool, *aghori*! Was one mistake not enough for you?'

'Evidently not.' Alex's lips twitched, but Beth did not think it was in amusement. 'Like you, Papa, I am not infallible.'

'Tch!'

Constantine snorted his disgust, and although Beth would willingly have given him his way she had discovered how strong Alex's fingers could be. His grip might be loose, but it was inflexible, and she had no choice but to stay where she was.

And then Linda appeared, bringing a welcome release of tension, and Beth was free. And, before she had time to feel any relief at this sudden change of status, she encountered Constantine's inimical stare. While Alex went to meet his son's wife, treating her with the utmost courtesy, his father had no such delicacy.

'Have a care, Miss Haley,' he said, before she could turn away. 'I can be a good friend. I am not a good enemy.'

Beth hadn't thought she would enjoy anything after that, but she was wrong. In spite of the fact that Alex made no further attempt to treat her any differently than he had done the day before—and did she really want him to?—he was a fascinating tour guide, and knew all the myths and legends associated with this particular corner of his country. That he knew a great deal more than that she had no doubts, but he confined himself to what was near and familiar.

They started in the village of Vouliari, and Beth, seated discreetly in the back of the sleek Mercedes convertible, couldn't help but notice how easily Alex spoke to the people. Even the children danced along beside the car, shouting words of greeting, little girls giggling merrily when he made some flattering response.

The village itself was clean and spare, in the way of Greek architecture, with white-painted stone dwellings clinging to the slopes above the harbour. A few boats nudged the stone jetty, their sails reefed, their nets spread over the stones to dry. Fishermen in patched jerseys, despite the hot weather, and cloth caps were mending their nets, and black-garbed women sewed and crocheted and gossiped as they watched the men.

It was a scene that was repeated all along the coast, but after a while Alex turned inland, and they drove past woods and camp sites and the rolling vineyards that marked this area of the peninsula. There was a gentle incongruity between the twentieth-century campers they saw, and the timeless indifference of a man leading a pair of oxen to market. But they all existed in an amiable melting pot, and there were few faces that didn't watch their progress with friendly interest.

They stopped for coffee at a tiny taverna, perched on the rim of an escarpment, where the scent of pine was strong in their nostrils, and where the air was sweet and cooler than on the coast. The little café stood among tall pines, and little wooden tables, with cross-membered benches, were set to take advantage of the view.

Which was incredible, Beth acknowledged, as she got out of the car. Below them, the hillside fell away in a lush terrace of vines and shrubs, with the lance-like spears of oleander exposing their scarlet petals. Between the trees, and on the mountainous slopes that rose at the other side of the deep ravine, the roofs of isolated dwellings could be seen, with here and there the bell-tower of a chapel, or the pillared pediment of some ruined temple.

'Beautiful, isn't it?' murmured Linda, coming to stand beside her, and Beth nodded, resigning herself to taking part in the conversation again. For the past couple of hours, she had been quite content to let Linda take centre stage, and Alex had inevitably restricted his remarks to the younger girl.

But now, out of the car, and once more under his eyes, Beth was aware of his appraisal, and although he appeared to be intent on summoning the waiter she was conscious of his guarded eyes upon her. What could he see? she wondered, making sure that the breeze did not mould the loose tunic against her body. Only her bare arms, and her legs, and the concealing fall of hair against her cheek.

Later, they sat at one of the wooden tables, drinking home-made lemonade spiced with cinnamon. The breeze was welcome now, lifting Beth's hair, and mitigating the sun's unguarded radiance. But it was hot upon her shoulders, and she smoothed her hand across her skin. Hot, and sensual, she thought, looking at Alex. Oh, God, she wasn't falling in love with him, was she? She couldn't allow that to happen. Aside from anything else, he was far out of her reach.

But, meeting his narrow-eyed gaze, she thought perhaps it was already too late. Was that why she had been so afraid, when he came back into her life? Had she really been attracted to him when she slept with him in London?

She dragged her eyes away, and looked down into her glass, striving for control, and heard Alex ask Linda if her lemonade was satisfactory.

'Mmm, it's lovely,' she answered, obviously not bound by the restrictions Beth was feeling, and Alex expressed his own approval.

'I'm glad you're enjoying yourself,' he added. 'It's been a pretty gruelling couple of months for both of us.'

'Yes.' Linda's response was more guarded now, but Alex had evidently decided to press his advantage.

'So,' he ventured, 'what are you going to do now? Have you given it any thought?'

Linda glanced sideways at Beth. 'Well, get my degree, I hope,' she mumbled.

'And then?'

'A job, I suppose.'

Alex inclined his head. 'You wouldn't consider working for the Thiarchos corporation, I suppose?'

'Working for the——' Linda broke off. 'You mean *here*?'

'If you like.' Alex shrugged. 'I meant in London, actually. But it's your choice.'

'Oh.' Linda had clearly not considered this possibility, and Beth thought how clever it was of Alex not to offer any overt support. 'Well, I haven't thought about it.'

'Then do,' said Alex, draining the liquid in his glass. 'Shall we have another?'

Beth refused, knowing, in her present condition, that too many drinks created other needs, and she had no wish to draw attention to that. But Linda was only too willing to have more of the delicious concoction, and when Alex went to serve himself she pulled an expressive face.

'What do you think?' she asked, in a whisper. 'Should I do it?'

'Work for the Thiarchos corporation, you mean?' Beth was purposely vague.

'Of course.' Linda was impatient.

'That's up to you.'

'But do you think it's a good idea?'

Beth shrugged, finding it difficult to imagine putting her future in Constantine Thiarchos's hands. 'It might work out,' she said casually. 'It depends whether you want to continue your association with the family.'

Linda pressed her lips together. 'Because of what Tony said, you mean?'

'No.' Beth didn't want to be accused of taking sides. 'If you think you'd like to work for Tony's father, then you do it. You can always resign, if you don't like it.'

'Yes, I can, can't I?' Linda nodded. 'And I have— sort of changed my opinion of his grandfather. He's not at all like I expected. And Tony's father is really nice.'

'You think so?'

'Don't you?'

Beth bent her head, and pretended to be brushing an insect from the weathered wood of the table. 'I—hardly know him,' she lied uncomfortably. 'Oh—here he is with your lemonade.'

Alex had got another lemonade for himself too, and, seating himself opposite them again, he pushed the glass towards Beth. 'Would you like to change your mind?'

Beth took a steadying breath. 'I—no. Thank you.' She paused, and then, realising Linda was expecting her to say something more, she gave a tight smile. 'But—it was—very nice.'

'Very nice,' agreed Alex, drawing the glass back to him, and lifting it to his lips. He tipped his head back as he drank, and Beth's eyes were drawn to the strong brown column of his throat. The muscles moved rhythmically as he drank, and a wave of heat invaded her groin. Lord, had she really wrapped her arms around that same throat last night? Had she held him, and kissed him, and let him explore every intimate inch of her body with his mouth?

His eyes returning to hers had her making a belated attempt to hide her fascination, and, as if to gave her time to gather her scattered emotions, Alex spoke to Linda again.

'Tell me about your relationship with Tony,' he said, in a soft voice. 'I'm not prying. I just want to know a little more about the last few months of my son's life.'

Linda bit her lip. 'What do you want to know?'

Alex shrugged. 'Anything you like.'

'You want to know if I was responsible for him taking drugs, don't you?' Her sudden outburst was unexpected, particularly after what she had been saying to Beth in his absence, and Alex looked taken aback.

'No,' he replied at last, meeting her resentful eyes with calm deliberation. 'Beth——' He hesitated over the name, and then went on more forcefully, 'Beth's told me that he'd kicked the habit before you and he became—well, before you got together.'

'Yes, well—that's true.'

'Did I say it wasn't?'

'No.'

But Linda didn't sound so convincing now, and Beth wondered if she was having second thoughts, in light of what she had learned—or thought she had learned—of Constantine Thiarchos.

'OK.' Alex hesitated, and then proceeded cautiously, 'I can't deny I was appalled, when—when Beth told me what you had told her. Was that why you kicked against getting involved with the family? Because you thought we'd blame you?'

'Well, it did occur to me.'

'Hmm.' Alex frowned. 'But I gather that wasn't the only reason.'

Linda sniffed. 'No.'

'Do you want to tell me about it?'

Linda shook her head. 'Not really.'

'Why?' Alex was painstakingly gentle. 'You're not afraid to tell me, are you?'

Linda sniffed again. 'Of course not.'

'Then what?'

'It's not easy.' She glanced at Beth again. 'I don't even know if I believe it any more.'

'Believe what?'

Beth was aware of Alex's growing impatience, though he had himself grimly in control. But she could feel his frustration, sense how he was feeling. She didn't ask herself how she knew. That would necessitate admitting exactly how involved with him she was. But, for reasons she preferred not to dwell upon, she touched Linda's arm.

'I think you ought to tell—Tony's father—everything you told me,' she said softly. 'He deserves to know.'

'Do you think so?' Linda licked her lips. 'But what if—what if Tony was lying? What if the letters didn't say what he said they did?'

Beth could tell from the way Alex's fingers clamped about his glass that he was finding it incredibly difficult to stifle his reactions. And, because she had started this, Beth had to go on.

'What if they did?' she countered, squeezing Linda's hand. 'It might help—help him to understand Tony's—desperation.'

Alex's features were rigid now, and Beth guessed what it must be costing him to remain silent. But the wrong move could destroy what little confidence there was between him and his daughter-in-law, and, meeting his dark gaze, she saw he understood.

'I gather you're talking about the letters my father sent to Tony,' he ventured quietly, and Linda's eyes widened.

'You know about them?'

'I know *of* them,' corrected Alex evenly. 'Were they a problem?'

Linda swallowed. 'Tony thought so.' She paused. 'They always upset him. He—he used to read them to me, and—and they did sound horrible. But they were in Greek. I never really knew what they said.'

Alex said a word that was intelligible in any language, and then, after a muttered apology, he put his lemonade glass aside. 'Do you still have these letters?' he asked, making a determined effort to keep his tone neutral, and Linda gnawed at her lower lip.

'Not all of them.'

'But you do have some?'

'I have the one that came the week before—before Tony died,' said Linda reluctantly. 'He—he used to burn them. But I found it—and one other—in his holdall.'

Alex wet his lips. 'Do you have them with you?'

'I—I may do.'

'Do you?'

Just for an instant, Alex's control slipped, and, responding to it, Linda adopted a sulky expression. 'Why do you want to know?'

Alex took a deep breath. 'Because I'd like to see them,' he said, after a moment. 'Please. I need to know what my father said.'

Linda looked at Beth. 'They are Tony's letters,' she said, as if seeking her support, but, remembering her own dealings with Constantine Thiarchos, Beth couldn't give it.

'Tony's dead,' she said gently. 'What harm can it do?'

A great deal, she thought privately, judging by Alex's expression, but she couldn't let him down.

Linda pursed her lips. 'Well—if you think so.'

'I do,' said Beth, giving Alex a fleeting look and glimpsing his gratitude. 'Do you have them with you?'

'I suppose so. I remember putting them in my wallet when—when I went through Tony's things. They're probably still there.'

'At the villa?' enquired Alex evenly, and she nodded.

'Good.' His smile was tight. 'Perhaps you'd show me when we get back?'

CHAPTER TEN

BETH sat in the first-class compartment of the London express and stared unseeingly at the fields and hedges flashing past the windows. It was a vastly different landscape from the one she had enjoyed so briefly in Greece, but appealing none the less. If she had had any interest in it, she conceded. Right now, she could have been sitting several miles up in an aeroplane for all the notice she was taking of her surroundings.

The steward had been very solicitous. When she refused his offer of a full English breakfast, he had suggested a lightly boiled egg. And, although for once her appetite was practically non-existent, she had managed to eat enough of it to satisfy him. The coffee had been hot and welcome as well.

But her thoughts were all turned inward. She was blind to the passing scenery because she had too much else to think about. The rain-washed hedges of an unseasonable August could not compete with Linda's revelations. The flooded fields were just a fleeting blur. When you were contemplating emotional suicide, you didn't tend to think about the view.

Suicide . . .

The word haunted her, she thought. And why had she thought of that particular word, when so many others could have fitted the charge? What she was planning had more to do with saving someone's sanity. Her own private feelings were a very secondary thing.

But even so, she had no real conviction that what she was intending was the right thing. It might be the moral thing; the *honest* thing. But was it the right thing? She felt the baby move inside her, and pressed an instinctive hand to her belly. This was her baby, as well as Alex's, she reminded herself tensely. Just because it had been conceived without his permission or his knowledge, and kept secret for those reasons, did not mean she owed him anything.

Or did she? Hadn't she always felt a certain guilt every time she considered what she was depriving him of? He might not like what she had done, but in the present circumstances she didn't think he would care about the ethics of the situation. He had lost his son, his only offspring. And she could offer him—what? A replacement? No, not a replacement, she amended swiftly. Nothing and no one could replace Tony in his affections. Tony was his first-born son; he was unique. But she could offer him the compensation of another child, a child of his blood. A child who might give him a reason to go on living.

To go on living!

The bald horror of that statement was frightening. She couldn't conceive that Alex was even contemplating the alternative, but according to Linda he was. He was just a shadow of the man he had been, she had told Beth on the phone two days ago. He wasn't eating; he had lost weight. And, according to his manservant, he was drinking himself into oblivion.

Even now, Beth found it hard to believe. Alex had always seemed such a strong man, a man full of life and vitality. Tony's death had hit him hard, but he had appeared to be coping with it. He had handled the whole business with remarkable fortitude, and until Linda had shown him those letters he had seemed more concerned about her future than his own.

Of course, Beth had known nothing about what was in the letters. She had had her suspicions, of course. But her position had been such that there was no way she could get involved. Besides, she hadn't seen Alex alone, since that morning they had sat and talked at the hilltop taverna. All she knew was that their holiday had been cut short, and she and Linda had returned to England without him.

She guessed there had been a row. Linda had hinted as much. But even she had been in the dark at that time. It wasn't until later that Alex had talked to her, and explained the reasons for their peremptory departure.

Of course, Beth hadn't known about this either, until Linda had phoned her, the day before yesterday. So far as Beth had been concerned, her involvement in their lives was over. Alex had said nothing about seeing her again, after they were back in England. He had wished her goodbye with tight-lipped detachment, his mind clearly on other things than pacifying her emotions.

Beth caught her lower lip between her teeth, and bit down hard. She wondered now why she had been so surprised he'd kept to his part of the bargain. Had she really thought that night on the beach would make a scrap of difference? He had said he *wanted* her; he had never said he loved her. He had used her, as she had once used him, and then dismissed her from his mind, as he'd promised before they left.

Even so, she had waited for two full weeks after her return from Greece, just in case he changed his mind. She had told herself she was waiting to make sure Linda got her degree, but the tears she shed in private made a mockery of her excuses.

Nevertheless, she had been there to give Linda the news, when she'd phoned to ask what her results were. Linda had graduated, albeit just barely, and her reaction had been predictably defensive when Beth had asked her what she was going to do. She was staying with her foster mother, she'd said, until Tony's father could organise a job for her in the London office. She didn't know yet whether she would take it. She was keeping her options open, until she knew more about what was going on.

Which meant, Beth knew, that she was not about to make any brash statements about her future, until it was more secure. Linda had learned not to take anything for granted, and promises made on a sun-swept hillside might wither and die in a colder climate.

Of course, she couldn't know that what Beth was really asking was what Alex was doing. But it was enough to know that he was back in England, and had evidently no intention of contacting her. And why should he? she had asked herself, as she had reluctantly replaced the receiver. So far as he was concerned, their affair was over. With no hard feelings on either side.

And that was when Beth had known that she couldn't spend the months until her baby was born in Sullem Cross. The university dominated the small town, and it had too many memories. Even her own house had too many memories, and it was with tearful determination that she had phoned an estate agent in Norwich, and asked if he had any properties to rent on the east coast.

The house he offered her was ideal for her purposes. It was just a cottage, really, but it was clean, and well-furnished, and stood on the outskirts of a village, just a stone's throw from the cliffs. The sea that surged on to the rocks below the cottage was nothing like the blue-green waters that washed the cove below the Villa Vouliari, but it was all the better for it. There was nothing in the cottage, or in the grey waters of the North Sea, to remind her of Alex. No one to take issue with her identity as a recently widowed school-teacher. No one to offer anything but sympathy, when they eventually discovered she was having a baby.

The house in Albert Terrace had been left in her daily woman's hands. Mrs Lamb had orders to keep the place aired and tidy, and to forward any mail to her new address. She had thought long and hard about leaving her address with anyone, but common sense had won out in the end. It would be foolish to cut herself off completely. The house could burn down in her absence, and the police would have to have some way of tracing her.

All the same, she had been glad that Justine was away when she left. It would have been difficult to explain her reasons for not giving her her address, if she had been there. She still hadn't decided what she was going to tell Justine, when this was all over. The truth, most likely, she had mused drily. Justine was not the type to tolerate anything less.

And, in the event, it had been Justine who had put Linda in touch with her. In her own inimitable way, she had demanded, and got, Beth's telephone number from Mrs Lamb. When Linda had got no reply from Beth's home number, she had rung the Sawyers, because she had known that Beth and Justine had been friends. It was a natural assumption that Beth would have left knowledge of her whereabouts with Justine. And Justine had always had the authority to get what she wanted.

Beth guessed Justine was probably wondering why Linda had wanted to speak to her so urgently. But never in a million years was she likely to guess the truth. Beth supposed one day she would tell her that, too. But, for the moment, the next few hours were all she could think about.

She was so glad Linda had contacted her, even if the girl's reasons for doing so were so different from her own. To Linda, she represented someone who had shared at least a part of what had happened. Someone who understood how she was feeling without reproach. Linda could share her fears with Beth without recriminations. She didn't demand unnecessary explanations.

But, of course, Linda hadn't told her that right away. To begin with, she had pretended she was ringing to let Beth know she had taken a job with the Thiarchos corporation. There had been some reorganisation, she had explained. Alex Thiarchos had been given complete control of all overseas developments, and would be working permanently in London from now on. She was working in the public relations office there, she added, answerable to Tony's cousin, Nicolas. She had a place of her own, a small but attractive apartment, over-looking Kensington Gardens; she was earning a good salary; and she had reluctantly accepted an allowance from Tony's estate.

She seemed busy and happy in her work, and Beth was glad for her. If nothing else, Linda had matured a lot in the past three months. She had also learned that not all the Thiarchoses were like Tony's grandfather. Whatever had happened, she no longer trusted him.

And that was when she had told Beth why she was really ringing. Her news about her home, and her job, had just been padding. What she really wanted to talk about was Alex. And the fact that Tony hadn't been lying after all.

And, remembering all the things Linda had told her, Beth felt a churning surge of repugnance. Those letters from Constantine to his grandson had been everything Tony said and more. What he had not told Linda was that his grandfather had known about his drug habit. The old man had despised him for it, but he had used it, threatening to tell Tony's father if he didn't do as he was told.

What his real intentions had been, they would never know. Constantine had denied ever threatening Tony with anything. But Alex had told Linda that he thought his father had intended to use Tony to control him. It had always been a constant thorn in Constantine's side that he couldn't dominate his younger son as he could his older one. Tony had been graduating this year, and had been expected to go to work for Alex. Perhaps Constantine had planned to use him, to spy on his own father.

Whatever, the fact remained that Tony had been frightened of the old man. His one transgression had been to marry Linda. He had said he loved her, and he had persuaded her to marry him secretly in the register office in Sullem Cross. Now, however, Linda wondered if it hadn't just been an act of bravado, regretted as soon as it was achieved. He hadn't gained anything, just provided himself with another burden. And with his poor grades, and fear of failure, it must have been too much.

Which left the unpalatable conclusion that Tony could have taken his own life. He might have been in a desperate state of mind and driven carelessly, but no one would ever know for sure. The discovery that

Constantine Thiarchos had visited Sullem Cross the day before Tony died seemed indefensible. And it had caused a rift between Alex and his father that Linda doubted could ever be healed.

Since then, she went on, Alex had become virtually a recluse. He wasn't interested in his work; he wasn't interested in the promotion his father had given him in a desperate attempt to regain his love and respect. He had even refused to see his own brother. To all intents and purposes, he didn't care about living any more.

And that could not be allowed to continue. Beth knew *she* couldn't allow it to continue. Not if there was a hope in hell of making him change his mind. Linda was worried about him. His whole family was worried about him—and with good reason. That was why Linda had contacted her. She had wanted to talk to someone who wasn't personally involved.

A bitter smile twisted Beth's lips. If only Linda knew, she thought, as the morning train from Norwich to Liverpool Street neared the outskirts of London. If anything, she was more personally involved than any of them. She had a vested interest in helping Alex. She didn't want her baby's father to die.

Tears pricked at the backs of her eyes, and she caught her lower lip between her teeth. Who was she kidding? she asked herself painfully. The reason she was on this train had little to do with Alex being the baby's father. She was on her way to London because she loved him. Because she would do anything she had to, to change his point of view.

Of course, it hadn't been easy finding out where he lived. She knew his telephone number wasn't in the phone book. People like the Thiarchoses didn't put their numbers on public display, and his office was unlikely to give her his address. Consequently, she had had to invent a reason to ring back, and that was why her journey had been stalled for another day.

As it was, she didn't know if Linda had believed her, when she'd made the excuse of calling to ask if she would give her *her* address again, because she'd lost it. Her clumsy ploy, of pretending that because Linda had been out when she first rang she had thought of contacting Alex in Mayfair, had borne fruit, but she could tell Linda had been doubtful when she'd explained that Alex's house was in Knightsbridge, not Mayfair.

'Oh, yes. Aubrey Square!' Beth had exclaimed, saying the first name that came into her head, and Linda had sighed.

'No, Wilton Court,' she had declared, with evident misgivings. 'How did you know where he lived, anyway? I don't remember him mentioning it.'

'It—it was at the funeral,' Beth had fabricated furiously. 'I—heard people talking about going back to the house.' She forced a laugh. 'Thank goodness I didn't try to reach him.'

'You couldn't have, in any case,' Linda had responded flatly. 'He's not taking any calls. And, when I went round to the house yesterday evening, his manservant wouldn't even let me in. As I said yesterday, he won't see anyone.'

Which wasn't exactly the most optimistic omen for her journey, Beth reflected wryly. Alex was turning away all callers, and she had yet to discover at what number Wilton Court he lived. She was hoping it was a short thoroughfare, with few houses. But what if it wasn't? What would she do then?

Her ingenuity wouldn't stretch that far. For the present, the fact that the train was slowing as it approached Liverpool Street Station was enough. 'Sufficient unto the day', she thought, wondering if this was the best time to be quoting the Bible. It was Aeschylus who had said, 'The Gods help those who help themselves.'

She checked her appearance in the taxi taking her from the station to Wilton Court. Her navy suit and cream silk blouse were purposefully businesslike. She didn't want Alex to think she wanted anything from him in exchange for the news she could give him. In addition to which, the loose jacket of the suit hid any obvious evidence of her condition. Indeed, even without the jacket, she was still remarkably slim. She doubted he would detect the truth should she decide not to tell him.

'What number Wilton Court?' enquired the taxi driver, glancing round at her now, and Beth licked her lips.

'Oh—I—I'm not sure,' she murmured, feeling the colour entering her cheeks. She crossed her fingers, and gave him her most appealing smile. 'I'm afraid I've lost the address. I'm going to have to knock at someone's door and ask.'

The driver gave her a sympathetic look. 'That's tough.'

'Mmm.' Beth glanced ruefully out of the window. 'Are we nearly there? Do you know if it's a very long street?'

'Not very,' the man replied reassuringly. 'It's just a terrace, overlooking Cadogan Gardens. Do you have a name, love, and I'll ask someone for you? No need for you to go asking. You never know who you're speaking to these days.'

Beth was surprised. 'That's very kind of you.'

'No problem.' He grinned at her in the rear-view mirror. 'Do anything for a pretty woman, I will. My wife says I'm a real pushover. Now, who are we looking for?'

'Thiarchos,' said Beth quickly, before her failing confidence had her asking him to turn round and take her back to the station. 'The name's Thiarchos. It—it's Greek.'

'Course it is.' The man nodded. 'I've heard that name before. Something to do with shipping, isn't it? Wasn't the son killed a few months back in a car accident?'

Beth caught her breath. 'I—that's right.'

'I knew it.' The driver was pleased. 'And, if I'm not mistaken, the house you want is Number Ten. I remember noticing it when the kid was killed. Always reporters outside, there was. Vultures!' He grimaced. 'Can't leave anyone alone, can they?'

Beth licked her lips. 'I—suppose they have a job to do.'

'Yeah, I suppose so.' The man gave her a wary look. 'You're not one of them, are you?'

'Heavens, no.'

Beth was vehement, and the driver nodded. 'I thought not.' He brushed the thought aside. 'So, does that sound right to you?'

'What?' For a moment, Beth almost gave herself away, but then she quickly gathered her composure. 'Oh—oh, yes. Number Ten. Yes, I'm sure you're right.' She managed to pull a wry face. 'I'd forget my head, if it were loose!'

'Like all women,' agreed the driver cheekily, and Beth was still smiling when he turned off Knightsbridge Road, and brought the taxi to a halt outside a tall Georgian town house. 'Here we are.'

Beth paid him before getting out of the taxi. Her legs felt like jelly, and the idea of standing on the kerb while she rummaged in her bag for change was not on. Even so, she still felt decidedly wobbly as the taxi drove away, and she approached the iron railings of the house with a total lack of conviction.

What was she doing here? she asked herself. What could she possibly hope to achieve? If Linda couldn't help; if his own brother couldn't help, what chance did she have? She could hardly force her way inside by telling some iron-faced manservant that she was expecting his baby. Who would believe her? It was ludicrous.

And then, with that uncanny sense of being observed, she lifted her head. Her eyes travelled up over the curtained ground-floor windows to the tall windows of the first floor. There were three of them, and her gaze sped from one to another in swift succession, but although she was almost certain someone had been watching her the panes were blank and unoccupied.

She shivered, in spite of the humid warmth of the late summer morning. The rain had eased here, and a watery sun was making the pavements steam, but still she felt a cold finger of apprehension down her spine. What if it had been Alex? she thought, her fingers hesitating over the latch of the gate. What if he had seen her, and was already ordering his manservant not to let her in? What would she do? What *could* she do? Oh, she ought never to have come!

She glanced behind her, half wishing she had asked the taxi driver to wait for her. It seemed so presumptuous now, to come here uninvited and unannounced. She should have got his number, somehow, and phoned first. That way, she could have saved herself a wasted journey.

'Are you coming in, or aren't you?'

The words, spoken in a harsh unwelcoming tone, almost paralysed her, but she managed to swing round, grasping the railings for support. Alex was standing in the open doorway of the house, his dark face grim and unshaven, but wonderfully familiar. Her jaw sagged in trembling disbelief.

'Well?' he demanded, and there was a faintly truculent note to his voice now. 'Either you are or you aren't. What's the matter? Did I scare you? You should have warned me you were coming. I'd have made myself respectable.'

Beth shook her head. 'You—you saw me,' she said, recalling that uneasy feeling, and Alex's mouth twisted.

'Of course I saw you,' he snapped. 'That's why I'm here. Do you want to come in and tell me what you're doing here?'

Beth nodded. 'All right.

'Good.'

His tone had shortened even more, and she knew she had to stop staring at him as if he were a ghost. But the shock of seeing him wasn't just a mental aberration, it was a physical one, too. Linda hadn't been exaggerating. Alex did look ill.

'Well?' he prompted, and she hurriedly lifted the latch and opened the gate.

'Thank you,' she said, walking up the shallow steps.

Alex stood aside for her to enter the narrow hallway of the house, and as she passed him she smelled the aroma of alcohol on his breath. Smelled him, too, a sweet-sour odour of sweat and unwashed clothes. He hadn't changed his trousers and sweater in several days, she thought uneasily. His hair was unkempt, too. Dear God, what had he been doing to himself?

He closed the door and gestured towards the stairs, which went up at one side of the hall. Ahead of her, she could see a long passage with doors leading off it, and a Victorian-styled conservatory at the end.

As she went upstairs, she couldn't help comparing the experience with that other occasion at the Villa Vouliari. She had the feeling that if she were to fall on Alex now he would crumple like a pack of cards. He had lost that edge of lean muscularity. Now he looked merely thin.

And old, she added, glancing anxiously behind her. She knew he was just a couple of years over forty, but at present he looked ten years older. Even his hair was streaked with grey, and his eyes were narrowed and sombre.

'In here,' he said, when they reached the first landing, and he pushed open the door into a book-lined study. 'It's where I conduct all my business interviews,' he added tensely. 'I assume you are here on business. I can't think of any other reason.'

Beth took a deep breath, as he closed the door and leaned back against it. 'Can't you, Alex?' she asked, realising she was not going to get any help from him. She glanced at the broad desk that occupied the space beneath the windows, and which was bare but for a bottle of whisky and a glass. 'Well, there doesn't seem to be much business being conducted here, at the moment.' She picked up the glass between two fingers, and viewed it with some distaste. 'Was this what you were doing, when you looked out of the window and saw me?'

'What if it was?' Alex regarded her without liking. 'Be careful, Beth, I've let you in here, but I may not be so willing to let you out again.'

'Is that a threat?' Beth took a quivering breath. 'Or a promise?' She felt behind her, and found a place to rest her unsteady hips on the corner of his desk. 'For heaven's sake, Alex, what have you been doing to yourself?'

Alex pushed his shoulders away from the door, and shoved his hands into his pockets. 'What's it to you?'

Beth sighed. 'It's not worth it, Alex. Believe me! Nothing you do can change what's happened. Tony's dead! You can't bring him back. And don't you think you owe it to him to do the best you can?'

Alex scowled. 'Who sent you, Beth? Who was it got the idea that *you* might succeed where others have failed? Was it George? Was it Nico?' He made a scornful sound. 'No—damn, it was Linda, wasn't it? So she did know where you were! The little bitch! She swore to me she didn't know where you'd gone.

Beth blinked. 'No one sent me,' she declared, even as her brain tried to deal with the import of what he had just told her. Had he tried to contact her, after all?

'I don't believe you.' Alex was scathing.

'It's the truth.' And it was. Linda hadn't the faintest notion she was here. And, if what Alex was implying was true, she probably wouldn't approve either. 'I wanted to see you.'

'Why?'

'Why?' Beth was taken aback.

'Yeah, why?' he repeated, crossing his arms across his chest. 'I don't believe we have anything to say to one another, do we? You said it all—before we left for Greece.'

'Oh.' Beth lowered her shoulder-bag to the floor, and gripped the desk at either side of her hips. 'You mean about—about you not seeing me again, after we got back?'

'No.' Alex was brusque. 'I mean how you refused to go, unless I made that proviso.' His lips tightened. 'That was the bargain, wasn't it? That was why you persuaded Linda to go.'

Beth swallowed. 'Maybe.'

'What do you mean, maybe?' His eyes flashed angrily. 'Damn you, you know that's what happened. You kept to your side of the bargain, and you made bloody sure I kept to mine. Where have you been, by the way? Or is that still a well-guarded secret?'

Beth blinked. 'Why do you want to know?'

Alex's face darkened. 'Curiosity, that's all. Oh, don't worry, I've got no intention of pestering you. I'm not totally stupid. I got the message.

'What message?' Beth was getting more and more confused. 'I didn't send you a message. And I've been staying in Norfolk, if you want to know. I've rented a cottage there. On the coast, not far from Norwich!'

'Norwich!' He echoed the word impatiently. 'And I thought you were out of the country. No wonder Linda denied knowing where you were. Norwich isn't exactly out of reach, is it?'

'Linda didn't know where I was,' protested Beth urgently. 'Honestly. She didn't. Oh—she eventually got my phone number from Mrs Lamb, my daily woman. But that was just a couple of days ago. Because she was worried about you, and needed someone to talk to.'

Alex didn't look convinced. 'To talk to,' he echoed, and Beth nodded.

'Yes.' She stared at him. 'Alex—are you saying you came up to Yorkshire?'

Alex stared back. 'As if you didn't know.'

'I didn't.' She moistened her lips with a nervous tongue, and gripped the desk a little tighter. 'Why did you come up to Yorkshire?' She couldn't believe it was to see her! 'Was there—was there a problem over—over the inquest?'

Alex gave her a pitying look. 'OK, Beth,' he said, 'you're obviously enjoying this little tête-à-tête, but I'm not.' He came unsteadily towards her, but although she was sure he meant to threaten her he just reached past her for the whisky bottle. 'So,' he went on, examining the contents of the bottle with a jaundiced eye, 'why don't you say your piece and get out of here? I don't need your help. I don't want your sympathy. I'll go to hell my own way, and that's all there is to it.'

'It's not.' Beth stayed where she was. 'Alex, please! Why did you come to Sullem Cross?' She took a deep breath, and dived into the unknown. 'Was—was it to see me?'

Alex gave her an old-fashioned look. 'What do you want—blood?'

Beth lifted her shoulders. 'As I said—Tony——'

'Tony's dead and buried.' Alex's mouth compressed. 'You said it, there's nothing I can do now. I loved him, and I think he knew it. As Linda says, we'll never know the truth.'

'Then——'

'Yeah, right, you want your pound of flesh.' His mouth took on a self-derisive slant, and he lunged for the glass. 'OK, I came to Sullem Cross to see you. But— what do you know? The lady's vanished again.'

Beth slid off the desk. 'I hadn't vanished.'

'It certainly looked that way to me.' Alex tipped the bottle against the glass, and swore when he found it was almost empty. His eyes moved restlessly around the room, as if looking for its replacement. 'I didn't get the message the first time around, but I sure as hell got it the second!'

Beth licked her lips. 'You're wrong.'

His eyes swivelled back to hers. 'No, I'm not wrong,' he said savagely. 'I asked everyone I knew at the university, and nobody could tell me where you were. You'd made a pretty good job of covering your tracks, Beth. Even your friends didn't know where you'd gone.'

'I know.' Beth sighed, but when he would have brushed past her she put out her hand and caught his sleeve. 'Alex, why did you want to see me?'

He pulled away from her, and lurched across the room to a carved mahogany cabinet. Jerking open the door, he revealed a generous display of bottles, and as she watched with horrified eyes he selected another quart of Scotch.

'Oh, for pity's sake, Alex!' Abandoning her stance beside the desk, Beth went after him, and because she caught him unawares she was able to wrench the bottle out of his hand. 'Tell me,' she said, standing in front of him, staring at him with frustrated eyes. 'Tell me why you wanted to see me! I thought you didn't want to see me again! At least, that was what you implied, when we arrived at the villa.'

Alex glared at her. 'Give me that bottle!'

'No.'

'I said, give me that bottle!'

He went to take it from her, and would have lost his balance if she hadn't taken most of his weight. As it was, her face ended up pressed against the whisky-stained cotton of his sweater, and, although the scent wasn't pleasant, the nearness of his hard body was achingly sweet.

'Don't do this to me, Beth,' he muttered, trying to extricate himself from her arms. But all she did was drop the bottle of whisky on to the carpet, and clutch the waistband of his trousers with both hands.

'Do what?' she asked huskily, gazing up at him, and with an anguished groan he bent his head to hers.

His mouth was hot and feverish, and painfully urgent, his hands cupping her throat with unnecessary force. She wasn't going anywhere, she thought dizzily, as his anxious grip almost robbed her of air. This was where she wanted to be, for however long he wanted her, and it was not until the baby stirred inside her that she found the strength to draw back from him.

Immediately, he let her go, his hands falling to his sides, as if she represented some form of contamination he couldn't cope with. 'I'm sorry,' he muttered, raking an unsteady hand through the uncombed tumble of his hair. Then, his lips curling with undisguised mockery, he tried to dismiss what had happened with a few careless words. 'I never could resist a beautiful woman!'

Beth's insides rebelled, but, although the temptation to take what he'd said at face value tugged at her emotions, she had to be sure. 'And—and is that all I am?' she asked softly. 'Just another pretty woman?'

'What else?'

Alex held up his head, and now she could read nothing from his eyes. They were blank; opaque; and, although her heart was telling her it wasn't true, her mind was telling her something else. This was Alex Thiarchos, she reminded herself tremulously. Men like Alex Thiarchos could have any woman they wanted.

And, because there was only so much she could take, she nodded. 'Right,' she said, picking up her bag, and looping it over her shoulder. 'What else?'

She was going down the stairs, when a man appeared from the back of the house. He was a thin man, of middle years, in shirt-sleeves and a patterned waistcoat. He looked at Beth in some surprise, and then offered a polite smile.

'Can I help you?'

Beth didn't trust herself to speak. She just shook her head, and, as if sensing she was near to tears, the man came forward.

'I think you ought to come and sit down for a few minutes,' he said, his eyes bright and sympathetic. 'I'll make you a cup of tea. I don't suppose Mr Thiarchos offered you any refreshment, did he?'

'Oh, really——' Beth got the words out with an effort. 'I'm fine, really.' She sniffed. 'I think I'm getting a cold, that's all.'

The man looked sceptical, but before he could say anything more Alex appeared at the top of the stairs. 'What the hell is going on down there?' he demanded, and Beth saw to her dismay that he had another full glass of whisky in his hand. He started down the stairs. 'Mallory! When did you get back?'

'I arrived home just a few minutes ago, Mr Thiarchos,' the man replied, undaunted by Alex's aggressive tone. 'I was just suggesting to Miss—er——'

He looked at Beth, and she muttered, 'Haley,' in a low reluctant voice.

'Haley?' echoed the man in surprise, and, forgetting all about what he had been going to say, he looked incredulously at Alex. '*This* is Miss Haley?'

'Shut up, Mallory!' Alex came all the way down the stairs, and thrust his glass on to the polished surface of a semi-circular hall table. 'Miss Haley was just leaving.'

'But Alex——'

Alex swung round on him. 'I said, shut up, Mallory,' he snarled, and Beth, who was feeling in need of some fresh air, groped weakly for the door.

'But you wanted to see Miss Haley,' Mallory was protesting, as she fumbled with the latch. 'I thought you said——'

But that was the last thing Beth remembered before the dizziness she had been fighting engulfed her. Although she tried to fight it, the blackness was beckoning, and, with a little sigh, she slid unconscious to the floor.

CHAPTER ELEVEN

WHEN Beth came round, she was lying on a soft velvet sofa, in a room she had never seen before. It was an elegant room, not too large, but high-ceilinged, with another velvet couch facing the one she was lying on, across an Adam-style hearth. There were soft green velvet drapes at the windows, and a pale striped paper on the walls, and an air of peace and tranquillity that was much at odds with the scene she remembered before she passed out.

She quivered, as the memory of that scene came back to her. Dear God! Was she still in Alex's house? She had been so desperate to escape, and it was galling to think that her own body's weakness had betrayed her.

'How are you feeling?'

Someone, a male, moved into her line of vision, and she saw it was the man she had met earlier. What was his name? Mallory? Yes, that was right: Mallory. Alex must have deputed him to look after her, and then get rid of her. Was he the one who had carried her into this elegant drawing-room? Had he just been waiting for her to come round?

Shame, and embarrassment, had her levering herself up on her elbows, but Mallory pressed her back, with a gentle hand on her shoulder. 'Relax,' he said. 'Alex won't be long. He brought you in here, and as soon as he was satisfied you were going to be all right he went to make himself more respectable. Now—how about that cup of tea?'

'Just some water, please.' Beth swallowed. 'I'm sure I'm being an awful nuisance.'

'Don't you believe it.' Mallory's thin face creased into a knowing smile. 'We've all been praying you'd show up before Alex did something really desperate.'

Beth gazed up at him. 'You're not serious!'

'You'd better believe it.' The man crossed the room to pour some mineral water into a glass, and brought it back to her. 'Have you any idea of the trouble you've caused?'

'That will do, Mallory.'

Alex's voice was harsh, but mercifully sober, and Beth shuffled into a sitting position to take the glass as he entered the room. Her skirt rode up her thighs as she did so, and she hurriedly brushed it down, but not before Mallory had seen and admired the slender length of her legs.

'Will that be all, Mr Thiarchos?' he enquired, but Beth could tell by his smile that there was a genuine affection between the two men that went far beyond that of employer and employee.

'For now,' agreed Alex, coming to take his place beside the sofa. 'But we may want lunch later. I'll let you know.'

Beth glanced up at his words, her eyes registering the fact that he had evidently showered and shaved. The dark stubble had disappeared from his chin, and his hair was damp and gleaming. Instead of the crumpled trousers and sweater, he was wearing black chinos, and a matching polo shirt, and although he still looked pale his eyes were definitely clearer.

'Fine.'

Mallory offered her a cheerful grimace as he left the room, and Beth wished she could feel as confident as he did that Alex really wanted her here.

The door closed, and as soon as it had done so Alex dropped down on to his haunches beside her. 'So?' he said. 'Are you all right?' His eyes were dark and concerned. 'I didn't mean to upset you like that.'

Beth pressed her lips together. 'No, I know.' She hesitated. 'I shouldn't have come here uninvited. It was my fault.'

Alex shook his head. 'Don't be silly,' he said tersely. 'I behaved like a fool. I've got no excuse, except the fact that I've been feeling pretty low lately. But that's not your fault, and I shouldn't have taken my frustration out on you.'

'Shouldn't you?' Beth took a nervous breath, and put the glass aside. 'According to Mallory, it's all my fault.'

Alex swore, and then made a muttered apology. 'Mallory should keep his big mouth shut,' he declared harshly. 'Besides, he knows nothing about it. It's my problem, not his.'

Beth looked at him then, and, as if unwilling to meet her searching gaze, he stared down at the carpet between his spread thighs. It was obvious he was doing his best to hide his emotions from her, and, taking her life into her hands, she reached out and ran her fingers down his smooth cheek.

His reaction was violent. With a muffled groan, he lifted his hand and covered hers, turning her palm against his mouth, and pressing a hot kiss against her moist skin. Then, with equal vehemence, he thrust her hand away from him, and got abruptly to his feet.

'Alex!' Her use of his name stopped him from moving away from her. But he didn't look at her as she swung her legs to the floor, and got gracefully to her feet. 'Alex—would it make any difference if I swore to you that I wasn't hiding from you?'

'Don't lie to me, Beth.'

'I'm not lying.' And, as he still looked sceptical, she cupped his face in her hands: 'Listen to me. When—when Linda and I got home from Greece, I went back to Sullem Cross. She must have told you. I was there when she got the results of her exams. That was when she told me you were back in London.'

'So?' Alex's eyes darkened. 'Did she also tell you about the God-awful row I had had with my father?'

Beth nodded. 'Not then. But later.'

'Well?' Alex moved a little restlessly under her hands. 'It was a pretty traumatic time for me.'

'I know that.'

'Do you?'

'I do now.'

'But you weren't sufficiently interested to wait for me.'

'To wait for you?' Beth's thumbs stroked his cheeks. 'Alex, you never asked me to wait for you.'

He closed his eyes then, as if he couldn't bear to go on looking at her, but his words were raw and painful. 'I didn't ask you?' he echoed harshly. 'My God, what else was I supposed to do? You knew how I felt about you! I told you in every way I knew.'

Beth moistened her dry lips. 'You said you—wanted me——'

He opened his eyes again, and now they were stark and desperate. 'And that wasn't enough?'

'You never said you—you loved me,' she whispered, and with a groan he finally abandoned his control and reached for her.

'Would you have believed me then?' he exclaimed, sliding his hands into her hair, covering her face with helpless kisses. 'Beth, we'd only known each other a short time. And our—introduction—wasn't exactly orthodox. I wanted you to get to know me, really get to know me, before I laid that on you as well. But—God! You had to know there was more to it than just—lust! Believe me, I didn't spend two months and a small fortune trying to find someone I just wanted to—well, have sex with!'

Beth was trembling so much, she knew that if he hadn't been supporting her, her knees would have given way. 'But you didn't come,' she protested. 'I waited two weeks!'

'Two?' Alex gazed down at her with incredulous eyes. 'My God! I didn't know there was a time limit. I really thought I had all the time in the world. And I had to get things organised here.'

Beth swallowed. 'I was sure you weren't coming.'

Alex brushed her mouth with his. 'It mattered?'

'Of course it mattered.' Beth gazed up at him half tearfully. 'Oh, Alex, I so desperately wanted to see you. And when I came here today——'

Alex kissed her again, more forcefully this time, his tongue slipping easily between her teeth, and searching every moist contour of her mouth. 'Today,' he said huskily, when he released her mouth to explore the sensitive hollows of her ear, 'today you saw a man at the end of his tether. A man who hadn't the sense to believe what was staring him in the face. Oh, darling, I didn't dare accept that you'd come for any other reason than that Linda had persuaded you. Don't forget I had to persuade you to go to Greece.'

'Oh, Alex!'

'And,' he added ruefully, 'I have to admit I wasn't totally immune to my father's poison myself.'

'Your father?'

'Yes.' Alex grimaced. 'At the end of our confrontation, he informed me that a woman like you would never settle for something as simple as marriage to me. You were far too intelligent; far too ambitious. That's why, when I found you'd disappeared again, I really gave up hope.'

'Alex!' With a little sob, she wound her arms around his neck, and pressed herself against him. 'He was so wrong!'

'Was he?' Alex looked down at her with searching eyes. 'I'm not a total chauvinist, you know. I'm quite prepared for you to go on with your career. So long as it's a little nearer London, hmm? I don't think I could live with there being a couple of hundred miles between us.'

She shook her head. 'I love you.'

'I hope so,' he agreed. 'Whatever happens now, I'll never let you go again.'

But would he forgive her? Beth wondered some time later, as she lay beside him on the sofa. Propping herself up on one elbow, she watched him as he slept. In sleep,

the lines that had appeared in her absence were almost
smoothed away, and although their lovemaking had
exhausted him he looked very contented now.

And that pleased her. It pleased her enormously that
she was responsible for him enjoying the first real sleep
he had had for weeks. He had told her that that was
why he had started drinking: because he hadn't been able
to get any rest. But one thing had led to another, and
the depression he had suffered had simply fed upon itself.

All the same, she couldn't help worrying about what
she had to tell him. She had tried to do so, before he
made love to her, but she hadn't had much success. Alex
had been hungry for her; they had been hungry for one
another. That was why they were lying here, instead of
safely in his bed.

Not that Mallory would come back uninvited, Alex
had assured her. He would be only too relieved that she
was here to save Alex from himself. Besides, he had
added, he didn't care who saw them. He was in love with
her, and he was going to marry her, and that was all
there was to it.

But would he still want to marry her, when he found
out what she had done? she asked herself for the ump-
teenth time. It had seemed so simple, coming here, because that was all she thought she had to offer. Now she
knew different, and she was afraid of what she might
lose.

Alex stirred, as if the turmoil of her thoughts had
transmitted itself to him, and opened one eye. He was
slumped on his stomach beside her, still wearing his
trousers, but without them being fastened. And she saw,
as he rolled on to his side, the coarse hair that curled in
the V.

'Hey,' he said, putting up one hand, and looping it
round her neck, 'did I sleep long?'

'Not too long,' she told him, turning her lips against
his wrist. 'How do you feel? Are you still tired?'

'Tired, yes. But I feel bloody marvellous!' he replied,
with a lazy grin. 'Come here, and I'll show you.'

But Beth resisted his efforts to pull her down to him, and instead ran a tentative hand down his chest. Beneath the polo shirt, his nipples hardened automatically, and she felt his thickening maleness against her hip.

'Come here,' he said again, his voice matching the urgent heat of his emotions, but Beth only shook her head.

'We have to talk,' she said firmly, even though she ached to give in to him. 'There's something I've got to tell you. The—the real reason why I came.'

Alex's eyes narrowed. 'The real reason?' he echoed. 'I thought you came because you wanted to see me.'

'I did.' She gazed at him uncertainly, and then hastened on before she chickened out. 'But there's something else you have to know, before we go any further.'

Alex pushed himself up against the cushions. 'Before we go any further?' he echoed, and his voice was wary now. 'How the hell much further can we go, Beth? Forgive me, but didn't we just make love here? What else can we do, except do it all over again?'

Beth heaved a sigh. 'Don't get angry——'

'Tell me what it is, and I'll try not to,' he retorted. 'Come on, Beth, don't keep me in suspense. If this is something to do with my father——'

'It's not.' Beth spoke hurriedly. 'It's to do with you and me and no one else. I—oh, what the hell? I'm pregnant! I wanted to break the news gently, but you're not giving me a chance.'

Alex looked at first stunned, and then incredulous. 'Are you serious?'

'Well, I'd hardly joke about something like that, would I?' she replied crossly.

He gasped. 'My God, you mean to say you're going to have a baby—*my* baby? Hell, Beth, why would I be angry about that?'

Beth sniffed. 'Are you pleased?'

Alex stared at her, still with that look of wonderment in his eyes. 'What do you think?' he muttered, leaning forward and hauling her into his arms. 'Dammit, Beth, of course I'm pleased.' He shook his head. 'Forget pleased—I'm bloody ecstatic!'

Beth's face broke into a tremulous smile. 'You might not be, when I tell you the whole story,' she mumbled, and he tipped her face up to his with a curious finger.

'Why not?' he asked. His eyes clouded. 'Aren't you pleased about it? Oh, no, this is going to interfere with your work, isn't it?' He ran a frustrated hand through his hair. 'There must be some way we can handle it.'

'No——'

'No?'

'No—I mean, it's not a problem. Not for me, anyway.' She paused. 'Alex—that's what I wanted to tell you. I wanted a baby. I wanted your baby—long before I knew how much I wanted you.'

Alex blinked. 'You wanted *my* baby——'

'Yes.'

'Let me get this straight; you were going to have this baby, whether I knew about it or not?'

'Yes.'

He shook his head. 'I don't understand.'

'It's a long story,' she said unhappily. 'That night—the night we first met—at your nephew's party——'

Alex gave an exclamation. 'Was that why——?'

Beth sighed. 'Alex, it's not easy for me——'

'No, but was it?' And, seeing the answer he sought in her face, he caught his breath. 'My God! I've racked my brains trying to come up with a logical explanation why you would do a thing like that. I never could believe that all you were looking for was some kind of kinky sexual experience!'

'I wasn't.' Beth's face was hot. 'I had this crazy idea about having a baby, and—and when I saw you——'

Alex was clearly staggered. 'But why would you do a thing like that? A beautiful woman like you.' His lips twisted. 'I'm sure there must be dozens of men who would consider it a privilege to be your husband.'

'Well, maybe.' Beth hesitated. 'But I didn't want a husband. I just wanted a baby.'

Alex's eyes were intent. 'Why?'

'Oh—the women of my family haven't been too lucky with personal relationships,' she murmured ruefully. 'And what you said—about how I look—that's always seemed something of a disadvantage. Until—until I met you, I'd never known a man I'd want to—well, to sleep with, anyway. I was hopelessly vain. Hopelessly naïve.'

Alex shook his head. 'You're not vain,' he said flatly. And then, 'I can't believe this. So that's why you disappeared. Didn't it occur to you that I might feel pretty bad about it myself?'

Beth sniffed. 'I guessed you'd be mad.'

'I was angry, yes,' he conceded. 'Wouldn't you have been, if I'd done that to you?' He smoothed his thumbs across her flushed cheeks. 'But mostly I felt—responsible.'

'Responsible?'

'Yes.' He sighed. 'Beth, you'd never been with a man before. How do you think I felt?'

Beth pulled a wry face. 'I guess I was pretty pathetic as a seducer, wasn't I?'

'I wouldn't say that.' Alex's mouth took on a decidedly sensual slant. 'I didn't just want to find you because you'd made me look a fool, you know.'

Beth looked at him through her lashes. 'Didn't you?'

'You know I didn't.'

'I'm so glad you did. Find me, I mean.'

'Yeah.' Alex closed his eyes for a moment. 'Me, too.' Then he looked down at her again. 'I must say you didn't look too pleased when I turned up at Linda's house.'

'I was scared,' she said defensively. 'I thought after—after what had happened that if you found out about the baby you might try to take it away from me.'

Alex made a strangled sound. 'That's some opinion you had of your baby's father, isn't it?'

'Well—you're a Thiarchos.'

'So?'

'So—men like you don't get seriously involved with women like me.'

'Don't they?' Alex's voice was teasing now, and she gave him a nervous smile.

'Well—not usually,' she admitted. 'So—do you forgive me?'

'Forgive you?'

'For not telling you before now.'

'But you were going to tell me today?'

She nodded. 'Yes.'

'Even though you believed I didn't want you?'

She coloured. 'You know I was.'

'Why?'

'Because I was worried about you,' she exclaimed fiercely. 'When Linda told me how—how you were—I was desperate. I'd have done anything to make you start living again. Even if it meant giving up the baby——'

'Oh, Beth!' He brought her mouth to his with aching intent, and then turned until she was lying against the cushions again, cradled in his arms. 'I've been through hell, thinking you didn't want me. If only you'd been there when I went back to Sullem Cross. We could have saved ourselves such a lot of heartache.'

'Mmm.' Beth stroked his cheek. 'But I knew I had to go away. The—the baby is beginning to show. Not a lot,' she added, as his hand probed the gentle swell at her waist, 'but enough for people to start talking. And I was afraid Linda might decide to come back.'

'And tell me,' put in Alex softly. 'Yes. That could have been awkward.'

'You don't think she'll mind, do you?' she whispered, as Alex pulled her blouse apart, and bent to lay his lips against her stomach, and he made a satisfied sound.

'Frankly, I don't care what she thinks,' he assured her huskily. 'As far as I'm concerned, you're the only person I care about. Now, tell me—when are you going to make me a father?'

Beth had never been to the Greek Islands before. And Kalos, the tiny island Alex had inherited from his Greek grandmother, and which he had chosen as their holiday home, was probably the most beautiful island of them all.

But then, she was biased, she thought contentedly, lifting a slim arm to take the weight of her hair from her neck. As far as she was concerned, so long as she and Alex—and baby Alexa—were together, anywhere was paradise.

Nevertheless, spring in the islands was a most attractive time of year. It was hot—but not too hot, sunny—but not too sunny. It was altogether delightful, and Beth knew they had all benefited from the break.

They had been staying here, in the villa, for the past three weeks, and although it had none of the amenities of some of the larger hotels it had been a wonderful experience. They had brought their own groceries, and cooked their own food, and after romantic evenings spent by candlelight she was not really looking forward to going home to the prosaicness of electricity.

Still, although they were flying back to England tomorrow, she wasn't really discontented. She was quite at home in Alex's house in Wilton Court now, and she knew Mallory was eagerly waiting to see how Alexa had grown in their absence.

And, at four and a half months, Alexa was developing quite a personality of her own. She was also quite demanding, which was why Alex hadn't objected when Beth suggested inviting Linda to come with them. The girl was good with the baby, and her presence had enabled Beth and Alex to have more time on their own.

Of course, they could have brought Mrs Summers with them, but Beth had wanted some time alone with the baby, and the nanny Alex had hired to help her was inclined to fuss. Still, she'd have been lost without the woman's assistance in the first few weeks after the baby was born, and although she still fed Alexa herself she didn't mind sharing the less attractive duties.

But this holiday—their first together, since their honeymoon in Tahiti—had been utterly delicious. Linda hadn't been intrusive, and she thought it was more than a passing coincidence that Tony's cousin, Nicolas, should have found several reasons to come and see his uncle while they were away. She suspected Linda knew perfectly well why he kept appearing, but for the first time in her life she was independent, and Beth didn't think she'd surrender that for a little time yet.

For herself, Beth couldn't imagine her life now without Alex. The past nine months had been the happiest nine months of her whole life, and she could only pity the girl she had once been for being afraid of reaching for happiness. Her mother's and her sister's lives had no bearing on her own. She was just so lucky to have found the only man for her in such an incredible way.

Linda had thought their story was really romantic—once she had got over the fact that Alex had been more concerned with sustaining his relationship with Beth than obeying his father's commands. The trip to Greece had been as much his idea as Constantine's, although the old man had taken the opportunity to try and find out what Linda knew about his letters.

Justine had shown the most surprise. Beth had certainly not lived up to her opinion of her, and when she had learned that her friend was expecting a baby she had been her usual malicious self.

'Better you than me, darling,' she had declared, when Beth had gone back to Sullem Cross to explain that she was going to live in London. 'And I'd have thought Alex Thiarchos's experiences with fatherhood would have put him off once and for all! But there you are; it's your life, not mine.'

And such a life, thought Beth now, getting up from the cushioned lounger she had been occupying on the veranda of the villa to wave at her husband and Linda, who were toiling up the beach from the shoreline. They had taken Alexa to dip her toes in the water—which she loved—and the baby was tipped over her father's shoulder now, blowing bubbles at the young woman who walked beside them. Alexa's *sister-in-law*, Beth thought incredulously. But it was good for Linda to have a real family at last.

Alex handed the baby to Linda when they reached the veranda, and heaved a sigh. 'I need a rest,' he said firmly, flinging himself on to the lounger Beth had vacated, and pulling his wife down on to his lap. 'Be an angel, and look after Alexa for the next half-hour, will you, Linda? I've got to build up my strength before it's time to prepare lunch.'

'Poor thing!' Linda pulled a face, but her eyes were warm as they rested on the pair of them. 'OK. I'll go and see if this young lady is ready for a nap. Then *I'll* prepare the lunch. So long as you don't mind something simple.'

'Whatever takes your fancy,' Alex assured her lazily, burying his face in the soft hollow between Beth's neck and her shoulder. 'So long as I can have the same privilege,' he added, for his wife's ears only, and Linda gave a resigned grin, and marched into the house.

'Alex,' Beth protested, but it was only a half-hearted sound, and he didn't take any notice of her. With her honey-tinted skin, and skimpy black bikini, she was totally irresistible, and his mouth sought hers with an eagerness born of need.

'I love you,' he said huskily, threading his fingers through her hair. 'I did tell you that, didn't I? At least ten times before.'

'At least a hundred,' she corrected him softly, settling herself against his bare chest. Like her, he was only wearing the minimum amount of clothing, and he looked lean, and muscular, and marvellously fit.

'Home tomorrow,' he murmured, against her hair. 'Will you mind?'

'Just us not being together every minute of the day,' she admitted ruefully. 'But I guess I can live with that. Alexa keeps me busy.'

'And what about your work?' he ventured. 'Have you thought any more about that? You know I won't in-terfere—if it's what you want to do.'

'Hmm.' Beth sighed. 'Well, I've been thinking about that too. But, if it's all the same to you, I'm in no hurry to get back to work. I like being your wife. I like being with our baby. And—who knows?—perhaps we'll have another baby. It's possible, you know.'

Alex shook his head. 'It's highly probable,' he muttered his hands moving possessively over her body. 'I just don't want to tie you down. I know how you value your independence.'

'How I *used* to value it,' Beth amended swiftly. 'I'm not like that any more. I suppose what I mean is, when you love somebody, you put their happiness first. I don't think either my mother or my sister ever had that experience.'

Alex's fingers caressed the nape of her neck as he kissed her. Then, with a sigh, he said, 'Talking of families, Nick tells me my father is desperate to meet his new granddaughter.'

'Is he?' Beth lifted her head and looked at her husband. 'And how do you feel about that?'

'I don't know.' Alex grimaced. 'Like you, I guess, I've mellowed during the last few months. I've got so much now. And who knows whether what happened wouldn't still have happened if my father hadn't been involved? Tony always was—well, he didn't take kindly to control. He was a lot like his mother. He was always wanting to try new things.'

'Like going to university in England?'

'Yes, that. And—everything else.'

'The drug taking?'

'Hmm.' Alex sighed. 'What do you think? Do we give my father another chance?'

'If that's what you want.' Beth snuggled down again. 'We've got nothing to fear from him. In some ways, I feel sorry for him. He lost something precious, too.'

Alex turned his lips against her forehead. 'I shall be sure and tell him that you persuaded me to forgive him,' he declared. 'You're good at that—persuading people, I mean.'

'You're not so bad at it yourself,' remarked Beth, sleepily. 'Hmm, isn't it hot?'

'It'll be cooler in our bedroom,' agreed Alex, lifting her into his arms, and getting to his feet. 'Well, the temperature, anyway,' he appended. 'I can't vouch for anything else.'

POSTCARDS FROM EUROPE

HARLEQUIN PRESENTS®

Travel across Europe in 1994 with Harlequin Presents. Collect a new Postcards from Europe title each month!

Don't miss
SUDDEN FIRE
by Elizabeth Oldfield
Harlequin Presents #1676

Available in August wherever Harlequin Presents books are sold.

HPPFE8

Hi!

Things haven't changed much in Portugal. In fact, Vítor wants to pick up where we left off. But I simply can't let him discover he's the father of my son!

Love, Ashley

MILLION DOLLAR SWEEPSTAKES (III)

No purchase necessary. To enter, follow the directions published. Method of entry may vary. For eligibility, entries must be received no later than March 31, 1996. No liability is assumed for printing errors, lost, late or misdirected entries. Odds of winning are determined by the number of eligible entries distributed and received. Prizewinners will be determined no later than June 30, 1996.

Sweepstakes open to residents of the U.S. (except Puerto Rico), Canada, Europe and Taiwan who are 18 years of age or older. All applicable laws and regulations apply. Sweepstakes offer void wherever prohibited by law. Values of all prizes are in U.S. currency. This sweepstakes is presented by Torstar Corp., its subsidiaries and affiliates, in conjunction with book, merchandise and/or product offerings. For a copy of the Official Rules send a self-addressed, stamped envelope (WA residents need not affix return postage) to: MILLION DOLLAR SWEEPSTAKES (III) Rules, P.O. Box 4573, Blair, NE 68009, USA.

EXTRA BONUS PRIZE DRAWING

No purchase necessary. The Extra Bonus Prize will be awarded in a random drawing to be conducted no later than 5/30/96 from among all entries received. To qualify, entries must be received by 3/31/96 and comply with published directions. Drawing open to residents of the U.S. (except Puerto Rico), Canada, Europe and Taiwan who are 18 years of age or older. All applicable laws and regulations apply; offer void wherever prohibited by law. Odds of winning are dependent upon number of eligibile entries received. Prize is valued in U.S. currency. The offer is presented by Torstar Corp., its subsidiaries and affiliates in conjunction with book, merchandise and/or product offering. For a copy of the Official Rules governing this sweepstakes, send a self-addressed, stamped envelope (WA residents need not affix return postage) to: Extra Bonus Prize Drawing Rules, P.O. Box 4590, Blair, NE 68009, USA.

SWP-H794

HARLEQUIN®

PRESENTS *plus*

When Cyn discovers that her latest client's future groom
is Wolf Thornton, the man *she'd* once
intended to marry, she begins to dream about a
return engagement.

Laura's fiancé, Patrick, is a true romantic *and* he likes
to cook. So why is she falling in love with Josh Kern, a
man who is Patrick's complete opposite?

Fall in love with Wolf and Josh—Cyn and Laura do!

Watch for

Return Engagement by Carole Mortimer
Harlequin Presents Plus #1671

and

Falling in Love by Charlotte Lamb
Harlequin Presents Plus #1672

Harlequin Presents Plus
The best has just gotten better!

Available in August wherever Harlequin books are sold.